SANE GRACE

Gray Door Ltd.

ISBN 978-1-945530-09-8

CONTENTS

CHAPTER ONE:

GOOD WITCH
OR BAD WITCH?

2054, San Antonio, capital of the central region, Commonwealth of the Americas. The Ghetto District.

"So … I just need to hit those little balls into the pocket thingies, and I get the money?"

Grace examined the slightly glowing pool cue with a confused expression. Nine men sat, stood or leaned against the wall of the notorious and smoke-filled "8th Street Tavern." As a holographic band played a classic techno-tune in the far corner of the establishment, the men watched Grace with hunger-filled eyes.

The woman of twenty-five was a beautiful brunette. She wore a tight-fitting, short skirt with neon-green fishnet stockings. As she held up the pool cue and attempted to position it as one of the men showed her, she leaned over, and they all maneuvered in a manner to get a better view of her ample cleavage. The low-cut and tight-fitting top seemed to barely hold Grace's buxom assets in.

A tall man with a mustache and goatee moved close to her. He wore a leather jacket and appeared to be the leader.

"That's it. Easy as can be! But like I told you, sugar, first you've got to break the balls."

Grace giggled, stood back straight and put her hand to her mouth.

"I'm sorry, but that's funny. I know something about breaking balls, but not like this!"

The men chuckled. The leader looked around the dimly lit room and smiled wide as Grace leaned over the pool table again and tried to take aim at the cue ball. She stopped and stood back up.

"I don't know. … I'm not sure about this. I mean, I need the money but, if I lose?"

She looked at the leader, and he said, "If you lose, we get to have our way with you … for the next six hours."

Grace grimaced. She looked around at the men and then looked down at the man's communication device, which lay on the side of the pool table. She turned her head to read the "23,000" dollars displayed on the screen.

"Well, I'm a little scared … and besides that, once I return the money to Mr. Watson's account, I'll still need enough to get away."

The leader expelled a long breath. He moved around to face her.

"Listen …" He held out his hand in a questioning manner.

"Grace," she replied.

"Yeah, Grace. Listen, you came here to our little piece of heaven. You tell us that you've been embezzling your boss' money, and he's about to find out. You say you need 23,000 dollars real fast, so you can cover your ass. We've got 23,000 dollars here, and we're willing to give you a chance to earn it." He turned to the other men. "Right, guys?" They all murmured or grunted in affirmation.

The leader then turned back to Grace.

"But we are the Diablos. That may not mean anything to you, but our gang has a reputation to uphold. We would love to just give you 23,000 dollars and help you out, but we need to keep our dignity too. So, you play a simple game of pool against me. You win, and you get the 23,000. If you lose, we get to entertain you for six short hours. That's the deal."

Grace smiled a little. She looked around the room with a bit of apprehension.

"Yeah, but you're probably better at this game than I am. And I need at least a thousand dollars to clean my travel log. Otherwise, Mr. Watson will know where I went."

Again, the leader expelled a long breath, seeming to lose patience. He looked Grace over from top to bottom. Then, he turned to the others.

"Come on, guys … another thousand. Let's make this easy."

Several of the men stepped up and waved their comm. devices over the one on the pool table. The dollars jumped up until the last man saw it was 23,780. He tapped his device and waved it over the leader's, and the amount jumped up to 24,000 dollars.

"There you go, sweetheart, 24,000 dollars." He then smiled smugly.

Grace leaned over and looked at the device. "But it's still locked."

The man raised his hands in the air. "What, you don't trust us?"

"Well, it's just, if I lose ... I mean, there are ..." She counted the men slowly, pointing to each one. "There are nine of you! If I lose, it's ... well, six hours is a long time, and I'm just one woman! You've got to unlock it, or I'm going to have to say no."

The man expressed frustration. He rubbed the side of his head and then leaned back to examine her bottom. This appeared to reinforce his patience, and he stepped closer.

"Listen, Grace, sweetheart. You're already here, in the center of our little universe. It's going to be difficult to say no now." Several men chuckled under their breath. He continued.

"But we like to keep things nice and simple. So, for you, I'll make this one exception. Just remember, though, I'm going out of my way to help you, all right?"

The man picked up the device and tapped several buttons on the screen. The screen changed to a green background, and he set it back down on the table.

"Now, can we get this game started? Mr. Watson will be waking up soon. You want to get that money back in his account before then, right?"

Grace smiled. "Thank you." She turned to the other men with an innocent smile. "Thanks to all of you. I promise you; I won't forget this."

The leader smiled as Grace spread her legs slightly and again leaned over the table.

"Oh, we're sure you won't, sugar. We're sure you won't."

As she propped her arm on the table and moved the stick in an aiming fashion, she could see a mirror across from her. In the mirror, she noticed a man stand up, step a few feet behind her and begin to make humping motions. The other men laughed about this.

Grace frowned, turned just a bit and began swinging the pool cue back and forth very swiftly as if she was about to hit the cue ball. But, on a backswing, she let go of the pool cue. It flew straight into the man's groin with a thud. He went from making a humping motion to grasping his privates, then groaning, he leaned over.

"Ahhhggggg!"

"Oopsie!" Grace straightened up and turned around.

"Oh … oh, no! Did I hit you? I'm so sorry!"

She reached down and picked up the pool cue. As she raised up, the stick struck the man in the face, causing him to fall backward and onto the hard floor.

"Oh. Oops, oh, I'm sorry … again!" Here, let me help you!"

Grace took a step toward the man and appeared to trip. When she fell, her knee landed in the man's stomach.

"Ahhgggg, you … stupid bitch! GET OFF ME!" the man grunted.

"Oh, oops!" Grace tried to get back up as the other men laughed aloud. The man who was making the humping motions now rolled on the floor in pain.

"That's all right, sugar." The leader took her hand and helped her up.

"Will he be all right?"

"Yes, yes ... he'll be fine in a few days. Now, can we get this game over? The sooner, the better, right?"

Grace continued to watch the man groan and hold his midsection. Then, the leader handed her the pool cue.

"Oh, all right. Well, if you're sure he'll be okay."

"Yes, yes. ... Just make your shot so we can give you what's coming to you."

Grace again spread her legs a bit, leaned over the table and took aim at the cue ball. Just then, a jingling sound emanated from somewhere. She stopped moving the pool cue and looked down at her chest. The jingling sounded again.

The leader leaned over and looked to where the sound was coming from. He then said, "Your uhm," he pointed to Grace's breasts. "They seem to be making a noise. Is that normal?"

Grace straightened up. She smiled and looked down at her exposed cleavage. Then, she did a little dance that caused her breasts to bounce and jiggle. The jingling sound stopped.

"There, no problems!" She smiled and again leaned over the table in preparation to make the shot.

Once again, the jingling sound erupted from the area of her breasts.

Grace expelled a breath of frustration, straightened up and leaned her pool cue against the table.

"Excuse me just one minute, please."

She raised her finger into the air, then pulled on a gold necklace around her neck. A small cylindrical communication device was connected to the chain and came out from her cleavage. She then moved away from the table and touched the two ends of the small cylinder. The comm. device unrolled, and she held it up to her ear.

"Kǎ ēn xiān sheng de yún tūn diàn. Wǒ kě yǐ bāng nǐ diǎn cài ma?" After saying this, she glanced back at the men and smiled. They stood watching her with puzzled expressions.

"Lieutenant Wolfe, I know it's you. This is a highly secure network, and your communication device only works for you."

Grace winced at this. She frowned, and after a few seconds, replied. "Major Eneken, why is it you always call at the worst possible time? I have nine men behind me, all drooling at the thought of having their way with me for the next six hours. And I was really beginning to enjoy myself when, out of the blue, you call!"

"Lieutenant, I have no desire to hear about your personal life. And believe me, if it were my choice, you would never get a call from me. But for some unknown reason, General Thomas insists that I contact you and relay orders for a mission."

Grace shook her head in frustration. She glanced back at the men, then turned away and, in a low voice, said, "Can you give me five minutes, major?"

There was a silent pause. Then, the major said, "Five minutes, lieutenant. I'm calling back in five minutes."

"Thanks." Grace then touched the two ends of the device. It rolled back into a small cylinder with one end still

7

connected to the gold chain. She placed it back in-between her breasts.

Walking over and picking up the pool cue, she leaned over the table and, while taking aim at the balls, said in a much less innocent voice, "Looks like we only have time for a quickie, boys." She then struck the cue ball, and it slammed into the others. Three balls dropped into pockets.

"I'll take solids," she said while moving around the table. She leaned over and shot again, this time causing two solid balls to fall into pockets.

As the men watched in surprise, she made another and then another shot in rapid succession, then moved without hesitation to make the next shot.

"Eight ball in the corner pocket," she finally said, and then shot the eight-ball in. She then pulled an open comm. device from her pocket and waved it over the one on the table, transferring the money.

"Hey, bitch! You think you're going to hustle us? You ain't leaving here with our money! And we will have our way with you, but it won't be nice and gentle like!"

Grace stepped back as the other men stood up.

"You should all consider this a learning opportunity. Philosophically speaking, can you really hustle the hustlers?"

At this point, the men attacked her. She swung the pool cue back and forth, taking two men down in rapid succession, then stepped aside and landed her knee in the stomach of another.

Pirouetting around this man, she swung her pool stick and took down another one. The leader pulled a pistol from his jacket, but before he could aim it, Grace kicked it out of his hand. Then, she jabbed the pool cue into his gut, causing him to fall over in pain.

Without missing a beat, she kicked another to the wall, then rolled over the pool table to evade a man who was charging her. She punched another out with her free hand, then knocked one out with the pool cue.

Grace pulled her short skirt back down a bit and walked toward the exit.

The man she evaded looked at his friends lying unconscious or writhing in pain. He hesitated briefly but then picked up a pool cue and ran toward her. She turned, and as he swung his pool cue, she blocked it with her cue, which spun it around quickly, causing it to fly from his hands. She stepped up to him as he stood in shock. Grace handed the man her pool cue. He looked at it. She smiled and then punched the man in the face, who fell to the floor unconscious.

She waved her hand a bit from the pain of hitting the man and then turned again toward the exit.

The manager stepped from around the bar, examining the nine men laying on the floor in agony. The other patrons stood or sat with shocked expressions. The music continued to play as she moved toward the door and the manager.

Taking the comm. device out, she punched in a couple of numbers and then waved it across the pocket of the wide-eyed manager. A bleeping sound came from the device in his pocket as it lit up.

"There's a little something for the mess."

Grace then walked out the door.

As she moved down the dimly lit walkway, a hovercar drifted past on the street. Then, a classic wheeled cruiser slowed and moved by. Several men yelled out obscene offers to her. She smiled but continued walking. She then ducked down a dark alley, past a small group of people smoking drugs. Shortly afterward, she came out on another dusky street.

Rays of sunlight found their way through a few openings but barely penetrated to the sub-level district, which was several stories deep. Streetlights were the constant form of light in the old ghetto areas. A weathered and defective "recreational drugs," business sign blinked on and off.

A bit farther and moving past a liquor store, she noticed a flyer in the window indicating imported alien drinks such as "Kelluargan wine," and "Aventian lostria," to be on sale.

A man standing outside the establishment turned and said, "Hey, baby."

As Grace continued approaching her street-glider, she noticed someone squatting close to it. The man held a small device in his hands and was obviously attempting to break the security and steal her ride.

Suddenly, a holographic guard dog appeared by the glider. The man quickly scrambled back as an authoritative voice shouted, "Warning, this property protected by PIT BULL!" The holographic dog snapped at the man who had by now moved several feet away.

Grace stood watching. As the security system automatically shut back down and the holographic pit bulldog disappeared, the man again slithered up to the glider and returned to his attempt to break the protective system.

Moving up silently behind the man, she tapped his left shoulder. As he looked to the left, she reached down on his right side and snatched the device from his grasp.

"HEY!" The man turned around. "Hey, bitch, give that back!"

Grace smiled with glee. "Well, look at this! A Hacker 5000! I've always wanted one of these!"

The man stood up and moved toward her. Grace stepped back, lifted her leg and jabbed her high-heeled boot into his chest, then pushed him back and against a wall. The man grunted in pain as he slid down to the sidewalk.

Grace punched a few numbers into the console of her glider, and the power lock disengaged. She then quickly tapped information into the Hacker to keep it unlocked.

As the man got back to his feet, she examined the hacking device curiously.

"You better give that back, bitch! I'll kill you if you don't!"

She looked over to the man, who still rubbed his chest in pain.

"What do you think? If someone takes something from a thief, is it really stealing?"

The man reached into his jacket and pulled out a short metal pipe. Raising it, he moved toward her. As he swung, she stepped back and grabbed his wrist with her free hand, then twisted it around. To avoid a broken arm, the man moved around in a circle with his back toward Grace. He dropped the metal pipe from the awkward position. She then put her boot to his rear and pushed him headfirst against the wall again.

As the would-be thief rubbed his sore head and tried to collect himself, Grace reached down and picked up the pipe, then sat it and the Hacker 5000 on the seat of her ride. She then pulled the gold chain from her cleavage, and detaching the small cylinder, placed it into a holding socket on the glider console.

She turned and glanced at the would-be thief, then touched several buttons on the console screen. A thin rod lifted from the vehicle. Once the rod was extended to a few inches over Grace's head, a holographic image lit up. The display was a shower curtain that went all the way around Grace and her glider. On the outside of the curtain, the image of a woman would peek out from time to time. She held the shower curtain over her chest area and would wave her finger as if chastising would-be peeping Toms.

Being covered by the holographic curtain, Grace began to get undressed. Though no one could see into her privacy curtain, she could see out. As she took her clothes off, she continued to keep a close eye on the man who had attempted to steal her glider. He sat on the ground staring at the holographic curtain.

A jingling sound issued from the console on her street-glider just as Grace was stripped down to her underwear. The screen lit up, and she saw the image of Major Eneken. The officer, who was fifty-something, with clean-cut, graying hair along with a thin mustache, became surprised and obviously embarrassed by the sight of a barely clothed Grace.

"Lieutenant, do you not know how to place your display in privacy mode?"

Grace was turned away from him, watching the thief.

"Uhmm, no major. ... I never use that option. How do I do that?"

The major shook his head.

Grace reached over and picked up the metal pipe as the thief stood up, reached into his jacket and this time pulled out a knife.

"Excuse me just one second, major."

As the thief raised the knife and moved toward the holographic curtain, Grace took aim with the metal pipe and threw it as the man came a few feet from her. The pipe hit the man on the head with a thud. He staggered back a step and then fell to the ground, unconscious.

Grace turned back around, and the major got the full view of Grace wearing only her sheer undergarments. He held his hand up.

"Lieutenant!" He then reached over and touched something; the screen went dark.

"What is it, major? Where did you go?"

A disgruntled groan came from the console.

Grace pulled a sleek, black outfit with a corset-styled top from a compartment of her glider. As she dressed, the major talked.

"Lieutenant, you must be at the Americas Trade Headquarters in Vancouver at twelve o'clock for a high priority meeting."

Grace adjusted the outfit on her body, then reached down and zipped it up.

"I'm sorry major, but that's not possible. I'm in San Antonio, and I've been up all night. I'm very tired. You'll have to postpone the meeting."

Again, a disgruntled moan issued from the console.

From another compartment on her glider, Grace pulled two holstered, small automatic laser weapons and then strapped them around her lower waist.

The major finally replied.

"Lieutenant, there are representatives from all four world trade federations coming to this meeting. As much as I would love to tell the general what you said, I assure you he will not postpone the meeting for you. You are to proceed to the closest hyper-transit station and be in Vancouver at twelve o'clock for this meeting. That's an order."

Grace stopped what she was doing and looked at the darkened console screen. "Public transportation? Really, major? Do you know what a hassle that is? Not to mention what it does to my hair!"

The major replied as she pulled a long black trench jacket from her glider and put it on, then pinned the sides back to keep the lower section from being spread out.

"Lieutenant, I'm not the least bit concerned about your hair or anything else for that matter. My only concern is that you make it to the meeting on time."

She pulled several small items from the compartment and placed them in jacket pockets. Then, after a long pause for thought, she responded.

"Well, you tell the general that I'll be expecting lunch. I'll turn right around and leave if there's no lunch. Hyper-transit makes me nauseous if I eat beforehand, so I'll be hungry when I get to the meeting."

Once again, she heard a moan. Then, after a short pause, the major said, "I'll be very happy to relay your demands to the general. Perhaps, when you arrive at the meeting, he'll have sent word that you're not needed for this mission after all. Nothing would please me more, but my orders are to make sure you arrive at the meeting, so just be there. Anything afterward is your responsibility."

Grace shut the compartment on her glider and climbed onto it.

"Thank you, major, but I'm not getting my hopes up about being released from the mission. Obviously, it is highly critical if the general insists I be there."

The screen on the console became clear. The major had a puzzled expression. Grace looked at him and smiled.

"Yeah, well … for whatever reason the general has in mind, just be there on time. Got that, lieutenant?"

"Yes, major. I understand, and you be sure to pass the information on about lunch."

The major nodded with a bit of exasperation, and the screen went black. Grace powered up, then pulled the glider out to the street and was soon speeding toward an exit.

Twenty minutes later, she was walking into a large and very busy hyper-transit hub. She unpinned her long jacket, and it fell around her, covering her two pistols.

Strolling over to a line, she moved up behind a woman with what looked to be her daughter standing behind her. The young girl appeared to be around five years old, and once she noticed Grace, she examined her very closely.

Grace smiled and waved at the girl. The line moved up a few feet. The young girl then raised her hand and motioned with her finger for Grace to come close.

Once Grace leaned over, the girl asked in a soft voice, "Are you a good witch or bad witch?"

Grace stood back straight and glanced down at her outfit. She realized, with the long jacket and black corset top, she likely did look like a witch to the young girl.

As the line moved closer to the ticket dispersal unit, Grace considered the question. She then leaned over and answered the girl in a soft voice.

"Actually … I'm a good witch, disguised as a bad witch so I can infiltrate bad witch headquarters and put them out of business. But you must keep it a secret, all right?"

The girl's eyes widened a little, and she nodded. She then moved forward again with her mother.

A few seconds later, the girl turned and again motioned for Grace to come close. When she leaned over, the girl asked, "Can you do some magic for me?"

Grace stood up straight again and briefly thought. She leaned to the side and saw there was one person in front of the girl and her mother. After this person received their ticket, the girl and her mother would go through, and then Grace would be next.

Leaning over, Grace said softly, "Ordinarily, I don't do magic in public, but just for you, I'll make an exception." Grace then pointed to the ticket dispersal unit, and the girl looked to where she pointed. Then, Grace continued.

"After you and your mother get your tickets, turn and watch me. I'll raise my hands into the air and make all sorts of magical things happen, okay?"

The girl smiled with excitement and nodded.

The mother now seemed to notice that someone was talking to her daughter. She turned, and after giving Grace a suspicious stare, pulled the young girl around to her front.

The woman and her daughter stepped onto an area beside the ticket dispersal unit. It was a large square platform. Once they were on the slightly elevated floor, a light scanned over them from top to bottom. Then, the device asked for a destination. The woman said, "St. Louis," and a price displayed on the screen. The woman waved her comm. device across the screen and the transaction displayed complete.

The woman and her daughter stepped from the ticket dispersal unit. Grace then stepped onto the platform. The girl leaned over and looked back to Grace as the mother secured her comm. device. The light began to scan Grace from top to bottom. As soon as it got close to her chest, Grace raised her hands into the air. Immediately, buzzers and lights began to go off. A clear, but thick barrier shot up from the floor around the platform, effectively isolating Grace and containing her.

17

The girl said, "Wow!"

Grace smiled and winked at the young girl as the mother turned, and seeing the commotion, quickly ushered her daughter away.

Security personnel ran from different directions toward the platform with weapons drawn.

"KEEP YOUR HANDS IN THE AIR!" one shouted.

A few minutes later, a thin and obviously timid man, who Grace imagined to be the station director, approached the platform. He raised a device, and after reading something, looked to Grace.

"Uhmmm, do you have any weapons on you?"

Still holding her arms in the air, Grace said, "Yes, I have lots of weapons."

The man nodded nervously and then looked at the device again. Several seconds later, he asked, "Do you have a security clearance for said weapons?"

Seeming to lose patience, Grace said in a slow, deliberate voice, "Yes, I do have a security clearance for said weapons."

Fifteen minutes later, and after a thorough meeting with the station director and security officers, Grace was finally boarding a hyper-transit module.

She slid past a man in his thirties and sat down beside him. He glanced over to Grace with an air of interest.

As they buckled up their seat restraints, the module director began to go over the pre-jump instructions.

The man leaned over toward Grace.

"I get so tired of these hyper-jumps. My company sends me on so many. You know what I mean?"

Grace looked at the man, examining him closely. He smiled and winked at her.

Her face lit up, and she crinkled her nose with a cheesy smile. Then, with an exaggerated effort, she winked back at him.

The man smiled as Grace replied with an excited, girlish voice.

"Yeah, I know what you mean. I thought I hated flying until I had to stop due to my snakes. Something to do with insurance liability. So, now I've got to ride these silly hyper-jump machines."

The man's face twisted a bit. She looked at him with a straight face. He chuckled and smiled a little.

"So ... you're in entertainment, I'm guessing?"

Grace reached into a pocket and pulled out a folded, plastic item. She unfolded what turned out to be a colorful shower cap. As she put it over her hair and tucked the loose strands in, she replied in the same voice.

"Well, not anymore. It's really a strange thing. I used to hate wearing clothes! And it was great for making a lot of money. Then, one day, I woke up and realized I hated being naked. So, I had to find a new career. Now, I'm a professional snake venom milker!" She smiled at him and continued. "You would not believe how many things snake venom can be used for! And I have to say, ya really can't claim to know a rattlesnake until you've milked it!"

As the man studied her suspiciously, the face masks lowered from overhead. Behind them, she could hear the hyper-engine powering up. Grace smiled at the man and then put her breathing mask on.

The man put his mask on as the module director sat in her seat and buckled up. Then, she put her mask on, and the lights dimmed.

From the seats, a gooey blob seeped out and enveloped each passenger. Once they were completely covered, the goo solidified. A few minutes later, the hyper-module burst from its launch point. For forty-five minutes, it moved at a mind-numbing speed. Then, it slowed and stopped. The module shifted to another launch point, and then again, it blasted away. After another forty minutes, the module slowed and stopped.

Once the goo had turned back into gel form and retracted back into the seats, Grace took her mask off. As she unbuckled the seat restraint, the man also unbuckled his.

"So, maybe I could call you sometime?" Grace asked with enthusiasm.

The man's face twisted again. "Well, uhm, I'm actually married and have three kids. But thanks anyway."

"Oh, well, that's all right. Most of my other boyfriends are married too."

The man stood up, and smiling sheepishly, waved and left the hyper-module quickly. Grace smiled to herself as she folded the shower cap up neatly and placed it back in a pocket. She then stepped off the transit module and into the station area.

CHAPTER TWO:

SWORDS AND MAGIC

As Grace moved toward the exit, she noticed a man in uniform holding a holographic sign that read "Lt. Wolfe."

She walked over to him and asked. "Are you looking for me?"

"Uhm, are you Lieutenant Wolfe?"

"I might be. Why are you looking for Lieutenant Wolfe?"

The man appeared puzzled.

"I'm to take the lieutenant somewhere."

"Where are you supposed to take the lieutenant?"

"I can only give that information to the lieutenant."

She looked him over with a keen eye.

"All right, you passed the test. I'm Lieutenant Wolfe. Now, where are you supposed to take me?"

The man nodded. "I'm to take you to the …"

Giving her a suspicious eye, he said, "I need to verify you really are Lieutenant Wolfe."

"Very good! You're on your toes today. That one gets most."

The young man smiled and nodded.

"All right, let's go." Grace began walking, and the man followed behind.

Once outside, he directed her to a large, black hover vehicle. He opened the door for her.

Grace started to get in, but the man almost jerked and closed the door.

"Ahhhhmm, I still need to verify that you are Lieutenant Wolfe."

Grace smiled. Then, she pulled the left side of her jacket back and stuck her left breast out toward him.

The man appeared surprised but then noticed the small round badge on the front of her outfit, above her left breast.

Somewhat timidly, he lifted a device to the small badge. It bleeped, and a holographic image of Grace, along with her credential's underneath, streamed up from the small badge.

"Ahh, thank you, lieutenant."

"My pleasure," she said and winked at him.

He opened the door, and she climbed in.

After a short flight over Vancouver, the vehicle landed in front of the Americas Trade Headquarters building.

Grace climbed out and made her way up the steps. Once inside, she cleared security and moved to the front desk attendant.

"I'm Lieutenant Wolfe. I was directed here for lunch."

The young man eyed Grace suspiciously.

"We don't provide lunches here, lieutenant."

He then pulled up an information screen that hovered in front of him.

"You're scheduled for a meeting in … Uhm, well, the meeting room was recently changed."

As the man said this, men in white uniforms began moving past the desk with food carts that hovered over the floor.

The man watched as several passed by. He then looked at Grace.

"Well, it seems I was wrong. Apparently, the meeting location was changed to a larger one to accommodate a catered lunch."

Grace replied with a quirky smile. "Really? What an odd coincidence!"

The man frowned.

"You can follow them to the meeting room."

"Thank you."

As the last of the food caterers moved past, she fell in behind them and followed the group.

Six floors up and through a maze of cubicles with administrative personnel, she followed the caterers.

As she moved through the cubicles and toward two large double doors, men leaned out to get a better look at Grace.

When the last of the food vendors moved through the two doors, a soldier shut them. Noticing Grace walking toward him, he expressed shock.

The young soldier stepped in front of the doors to block her. He then touched a communication button on his chest and spoke in a nervous tone.

"Uhmm, sir … I think she's here."

As the soldier eyed Grace apprehensively, a reply came from the tiny device."

"Keep her there. I'll be right down."

Grace smiled at the soldier.

"A welcome party? For me? How flattering!"

Soon, a man in uniform approached. He was in his mid-forties and stood several inches shorter than Grace. His hair was black but had hints of gray.

"Lieutenant Wolfe?"

"Yes, and you must be my welcome party," she replied with a bright smile.

"I'm Captain Bradford. We've been expecting you."

"Well, that is good news, indeed. I always hate when I'm the party crasher."

The captain seemed puzzled but continued.

"Lieutenant, your reputation has preceded you."

Grace became instantly excited.

"Really? That's marvelous! Please tell me all the details. I want to hear everything. The good, the bad, the naughty! Actually, start with the naughty and work your way back!"

The soldier tried to contain a smile, but the captain did not appear amused.

"Lieutenant Wolfe, I'm sure you know Major Eneken."

"Yes! I know the major. I had a conversation with him a few hours ago, though I don't remember much about it. Come to think of it, I was in my underwear at the time. Perhaps that's why it's a bit fuzzy."

Again, the soldier stifled a smile. Several men leaned from their cubicles, as the conversation was obviously becoming interesting to everyone within earshot.

Captain Bradford groaned in frustration.

"Lieutenant, the major, notified me concerning your arrival. He also notified me of your troublesome nature. I'll have you know, I'm the officer in charge of your mission group, and if you get out of line, I'll use every resource available to have you reprimanded."

Grace again became excited.

"Could you? Could you just reprimand me now? But please be gentle. The last time I was reprimanded, it left bruises. You may not believe it, but I am somewhat delicate."

The soldier behind Captain Bradford could not help but chuckle and turned away to hide it. Again, men leaned out from their cubicles to get a better look.

The captain turned and gave the young soldier a sour look. He turned back to Grace.

"There are representatives attending this meeting from around the globe as well as our lunar colonies. You'll have to leave your jacket and any weapons you have here."

"Oh, very well then."

Pulling her long jacket off, she handed it to the soldier, who placed it in a locker to his side.

Captain Bradford motioned with his hand toward the two laser pistols strapped to her legs.

She reached down and unlatched the leg straps, then unbuckled the belt and handed the two automatic weapons to the soldier.

Noticing several throwing knives in sheaths sewn into the legs of her outfit, he motioned for them also. Grace expelled a breath of frustration while pulling the knives out and handing them to the soldier.

The soldier then scanned her with a small device, which immediately lit up yellow and beeped, indicating she could still have something on her.

The captain and the soldier looked her over. The sleek, black outfit she wore was skintight, and they didn't see anywhere that she could be hiding a weapon.

"Do you still have any weapons on you, lieutenant?"

Grace smiled.

"Perhaps you should frisk me, captain. Or, I should probably strip down. ... No. Better yet, I should strip down completely, and you should both frisk me!"

The soldier smiled brightly with this comment, and more heads leaned out from the cubicles in apparent anticipation.

The captain shook his head in frustration. He stood, looking at her for several seconds.

"Could I ask you a question, lieutenant?"

She held her arms out. "Please ask me anything. I'll reveal all my secrets to you. I'm an open file."

"I would just like to know how you not only completed special ops training but managed to acquire the rank of lieutenant?"

"Oh, well, that is an interesting story. You see, in the special ops training, there's a lot of running and jumping." She moved her arms as if running, then continued. "And, then there's the crawling around in mud and .... well, eewww, it's all very barbaric and repulsive. But, as it happened, there was some extra special training available that

26

I qualified for."

The captain appeared lost but asked, "extra special training?"

"Yes! Every morning after breakfast, I would go to one of the officer's quarters, and he would supervise some special exercises. I would take all my clothes off and then do some jumping-jack thingies and some squatting sort of exercise things for about thirty minutes. Then …"

The captain held his hand up. "Wait, wait, stop there. I don't want to hear any more. I don't want to know any more."

"But don't you want to hear about the showers? It's one of the best parts!"

"No, no. Just go in. But keep in mind what I said, lieutenant."

The soldier opened one of the doors, and Grace started to walk in but stopped.

"Uhm, just what part of what you said am I supposed to keep in mind?"

Captain Bradford growled and walked away. Grace turned to the soldier. He was smiling with glee. She winked at him and went inside.

A long table with a white tablecloth sat in a spacious meeting room. The scent of roasted meats drifted in the air. Caterers were busy placing plates, utensils and food in various areas.

Around the room, people stood talking. Most wore uniforms, though some were dressed in suits.

Moving over to a small table, Grace picked up a plate and

spoon, then stepped to the dining table and began filling the plate with green grapes.

A large and burly man wearing a European Commonwealth uniform walked toward her.

As Grace noticed the man approaching, she quickly stuffed several grapes into her mouth and pushed them into her cheeks, causing them to poke out.

When she turned back to him with her cheeks poking out like a chipmunk, the man stopped and appeared surprised.

After looking her over briefly, he did a slight bow and spoke with a strong Russian accent, "Captain Goryunov, European Commonwealth Commando Unit."

Grace pushed another grape in her mouth and examined the captain carefully.

"Corpheral Munnchkin. ... uhm, Thirhd Lancers, battalion ... X." She did a slight bow also and immediately shoved another grape into her mouth.

The captain's face twisted slightly.

"Uhmm, did you say, Corporal ... Munchkin?"

Grace nodded. "Uhmm, humm." She then started walking slowly down the table, examining the food.

The captain followed her.

"The Third Lancers ... I'm not familiar with that unit."

She glanced back at him, expressing surprise that he was still behind her. Then, with her mouth full of grapes, she replied.

"Iphts somtheng lieke ahh speecal ... uhmm, hoorse unet. Wee uusee, uhm, sowrds ann pikes annn yoou knoww ... aah, little magicc ... ann stuff."

Again, the captain seemed confused.

"Uhm, did you say you use swords ... and magic?"

Grace stuffed another grape in her mouth. "Uhmm hmm." She smiled and nodded, then continued slowly down the table.

He followed behind her.

"I didn't realize advances were being made in, uhm, 'magic.' Could you tell me more about it?"

She stopped and turned to him, then pushed another grape into her mouth and replied with less of a mouthful this time.

"Well, the reason you've not heard anything about it is that it's all 'hush-hush,' top-secret stuff. I'm not supposed to tell anyone about it, but I think I can trust you...." She held out her hand in a questioning manner.

"Goryunov," he replied.

"Yeah, I figure I can trust you, uhm, Gory...munudo. ... I mean, you're like a general or something, so you should be okay to tell."

She took another step, pushed another grape into her mouth and stopped. She raised her finger, chewed, swallowed, then continued.

"As it turns out, elves are best suited for crafting magic swords, but it seems they have a labor agreement that forced us to have our magic weapons made by the dwarves. I don't know if you've ever negotiated with a dwarf or not, but let me tell you, they are shrewd bargainers. That whole 'Snow White, getting off rent-free,' thing is really farfetched if you ask me."

The captain's face twisted as if he smelled something bad. He raised his hand.

"Uhm, well, this all seems to be far above my pay grade. I don't think I need to hear any more."

She pushed another grape into her mouth, then stared at him briefly before replying.

"Don't you want to hear about our new wizard regiment? The wizards, now they know how to handle a magic sword, let me tell you!"

Captain Goryunov examined her with a confused expression. He shook his head a bit and then walked away and moved to another side of the room to talk with a man in uniform.

Not far away, a woman who also wore an officer's uniform had closely watched Grace and Captain Goryunov. When the captain moved away from Grace, she moved toward her.

As Grace turned, she could see the woman approaching. The female officer was an attractive woman, but she also had a short haircut, and Grace could see the officer carried herself in a masculine manner.

Looking around, as if searching for a way to avoid the officer, Grace realized she was stuck.

The female officer stepped in front of her and smiled suggestively.

"I noticed you come in earlier. I was going to say hi when the gentleman began to talk with you. Men can be such bores, don't you think?"

Chewing her grapes, Grace finally swallowed and said, "Yeah, they sure can be!"

The female officer smiled with satisfaction, then Grace continued.

"That's precisely the reason I purchased an Omega-5, android sexbot."

The woman's face twisted. Slowly, a half-smile returned to her face. She lifted her head slightly, her eyes squinting just a bit.

Before she could reply, Grace continued. "In fact, I was so pleased with my first android, I purchased two more. They're super! No backtalk, endless energy and if you get tired of one, you just turn them off and stick them in the closet for a while." Grace smiled and added, "I recommend the Adonis model ... or the Vulcan XL. Either one, you won't be sorry."

The female officer almost appeared ill.

"Oh ... well, that's, uhm ... nice." She then glanced past Grace. Seeming to spot someone, she said, "Oh, I see a friend of mine. Will you excuse me?"

"Sure," Grace said and then moved back to the buffet as the officer quickly walked away.

Finding her seat around halfway along the table, Grace sat down. She picked up the small, folded name card that read "Lt. Wolfe," then noticed a plate, napkin and utensils, including a steak knife, were all laid out for her. Grace glanced back at the doorway and could see more people entering.

A distinguished man in a business suit entered from another door at the front of the room. He stepped up on a small stage and pressed a button on the wall. A podium rose from the floor, and as he prepared for the meeting, everyone in the room began to find their assigned seats.

A few minutes later, the man began to speak as the food caterers served the main course.

"All right, everyone, I'm Commissioner Welch. I apologize for any confusion with the meeting room. We were scheduled for room sixty-one A. For some unknown reason, the higher-ups decided to serve us lunch. So, we were moved to this room at the last minute."

Grace examined the others around the table as the servers moved from person to person, dishing out items. Eventually, when the servers were done, they left the meeting room, and guards stepped in front of the doors to block any unauthorized entry.

"Okay, we'll get this meeting started. Please continue with your meal. I believe we're all professionals here, so there should be no problem getting the information."

Grace ate her meal but also continued to study the room and everyone in it. As she was scanning the layout, something caught her eye. She immediately stopped eating. As the commissioner continued, her attention was drawn to the vent in the corner behind the commissioner.

"You've been called here today because our planet faces a crisis. You're considered the best of the best by your home federations. In this room, we have military, law enforcement, counterespionage, technical and other fields deemed critical to resolving the current threat."

As the commissioner spoke, Grace watched an odd, slightly shimmering, but almost invisible movement that seemed to slither from the vent to the left and in the corner behind the commissioner. Grace realized the mysterious movement to be some type of stealth device. It also obviously had shape manipulation capabilities, as it changed form to slip through the thin vents in an almost liquid manner. It then began to reassemble itself as Grace watched closely.

Before the device was completely reassembled, Grace realized something and turned away from it. She checked her pockets and then looked around her in search of something useful, recalling her weapons had been taken at the door. All the while, the commissioner continued.

"Since the earth became an intergalactic trading post fifteen years ago, we've faced a plethora of challenges. We've made lucrative trade agreements with friendly planets but have also had to defend our world from interferences and influences by not so friendly planets."

As Grace considered what to do, a man was let into the meeting room. The commissioner stopped.

"I'm sorry. I thought everyone was here."

The man moved sheepishly toward the table.

"Uhm, yes, I apologize for being late. I was informed the meeting would be in a different room. I'm Detective Vandenberg, representing the Antarctic Mining Colonies."

The commissioner looked over his information screen. "Oh, yes, I see you on our list now."

As Detective Vandenberg stood by a wall, the commissioner continued to examine the information on the screen.

"Well, it seems I must apologize again, detective. We

changed meeting rooms at the last hour, and it appears you are not on the table list."

The detective smiled meekly. "Oh, well, it's not a problem, sir. I'll just stand. I sat far too long during the transit here."

"All right. Well, again, I apologize, Detective Vandenberg. I was just informing everyone of a crisis. You've not missed much."

Grace searched her pockets. She pulled a small rolled item from one of them. The man next to her watched curiously as she unrolled a set of disposable sunglasses. She smiled at the man and put the glasses on. Then, she reached into another pocket and pulled out the shower cap, also putting it on over her hair.

As the commissioner continued, she glanced back to the stealth device. It was now a flat block that blended almost seamlessly with the wall. The device was so well camouflaged that she could barely see it. Once she assured herself it was still there, she quickly turned away.

"Recently, our planet has been flooded with the designer drug 'Fellirex.' It's cheap, extremely addictive and difficult to trace. It's common on several of our trading partner planets but only recently introduced on earth. With the market being flooded worldwide, we feel it will reach epidemic levels within a month. Law enforcement from around the globe have had no luck tracking down the smugglers. It's been suggested that several small smuggling groups have merged into one large and elusive group, but we really don't know. Therefore, you're here now. The world leaders believe we must go on the offensive before it's too late."

Grace examined the plate and utensils in front of her. She now felt certain the strange device was collecting information, and very likely, it was also gathering facial recognition data. As she considered this, she noticed the steak knife.

The man next to her expressed a bit of irritation, as Grace seemed to be paying no attention to the commissioner. Also, the sunglasses and shower cap she wore gave her something of a clown appearance rather than an expert of any sort. Yet, she expressed no concern for him or others who were becoming distracted by her activities.

The commissioner glanced at her, as well. He could only see the back of her head, as she was intentionally turned from the odd device that no one else had noticed. He paused for a second and then continued.

"The Inter-Federation Law Enforcement Association has managed to accumulate a number of leads, and we'll be assembling each of you into teams. We think there's not much time to unravel this situation. At the current rate of drug infiltration, half the population of earth could be addicted by next month. Since the drugs are coming in from trade points, this mission has been placed under Trade Commission Authority. As the majority of Fellirex has been coming in through the Americas District, the burden of stopping the flood of illegal drugs falls to the Americas Trade Commission.

"As you may also be aware, I'm in the process of running for the Office of Trade Regent. As the current trade commissioner for the Americas, I've been ordered by the global trade federation regent to head this task force. I'm hopeful we will resolve this threat before the election in five weeks."

Grace took her steak knife and, placing it on her finger, began to balance it to get a feel for the weight distribution. On the other side of the room, Detective Vandenberg took notice of her. He watched her check the knife quickly and, from time to time, glance toward the commissioner. The detective also noticed she wasn't looking at the commissioner. As the others were making efforts to ignore Grace's disruptive behavior, the detective became entranced by it.

Once she had a good feel for the weight distribution of the steak knife, she again glanced at the barely visible object on the wall behind the commissioner. He noticed her looking his way, as well as her now very odd appearance. She again quickly turned away from him.

The commissioner paused, looked down to the seating sheet and then, lifting his head, he said, "Uhmm, Lieutenant Wolfe?"

Grace scanned the table beside her and noticing a saucer of cream-colored dip. She reached over and poked her finger in it, then daubed it across her top lip, giving herself what looked to be a "milk mustache." She then turned to the commissioner.

"Yes?"

As she faced the commissioner and the strange stealth device on the wall behind him, it captured images of her to add with those of all the attendees.

"Lieutenant, are you getting this information?"

The others in the room examined Grace with disdain as she considered the question. She then smiled and appearing much like a clown, wearing her shower cap, sunglasses and daubed on mustache, replied. "Certainly, colonel, every word and detail. My mind is like a..." She waved her hand in the air as if trying to pull the words from it, "steel capturing device thing!"

The commissioner studied Grace. Everyone in the room examined her as if she were nuts. Then, the commissioner cleared his throat and continued.

"So, from here, you will all be grouped into teams. Your skill sets will be matched with other team members, and each team will be assigned to a specific lead the IFLE has acquired. It is hoped that this crisis can be resolved quickly and efficiently."

As the commissioner continued, the detective watched closely as Grace positioned the knife in her hand, as if preparing to toss it like a throwing knife.

Once Grace had the knife, blade first, positioned in her right hand, she looked around but didn't notice Detective Vandenberg watching her. The others were again focused on the commissioner and intentionally ignoring Grace.

Leaning back in her chair, she began to balance on the back legs. She wobbled a bit and managed to get the attention of those sitting close to her. Grace balanced a few more seconds, then appeared to lose her balance. She grabbed the white tablecloth as she fell backward, and the result was a chaotic crashing of dishes and food being pulled from the table.

Many of the attendees received a lap full of lunch while others had their drinks spilled on them.

Immediately, everyone stood or looked to the mess that was all around Grace's assigned spot. What they didn't notice was her rolling away from the disaster that she had created. She slipped behind a food cart, then crouched and took aim. Rearing her arm back, she quickly let the knife fly. Her aim was true, and the steel blade planted in the strange device. Glancing back, she saw that everyone was still occupied by the huge mess. Some were brushing themselves off while others attempted to pick dishes up from the floor.

Still crouching, she glanced back to the device and saw it lose its stealth camouflage. It then shook violently and fell from the wall.

Grace stood and walked over to the others who were, for the most part, covered with food or drink.

"Here, let me help!" She reached down and, picking up a half-full plate of food, raised up and turning quickly, slung it on the commissioner who had come down from the small stage area to try to assist the others.

"Ahhgg!" He glanced down at the mess on his suit. "Please, lieutenant, just step back. We'll take care of this."

He then turned away from her. Trying to wipe his uniform with a napkin, he side-stepped a large bowl on the floor and moved to help an officer who was covered with her meal.

Grace sat the dish on the table and backed up several steps. Again, ensuring all were preoccupied with the table disaster, she continued to move slowly toward the stage area.

Slipping over to the device, she saw it was attempting to regain its stealth mode and move from the floor. The knife was embedded into its body. She reached down and pulled it out. Then, noticing a piece of the device's covering that had come loose, she reached down and pried it away with the knife. It was a thin octagonal fragment that resembled an armor plate, but as she held it, the plate took on the image of her hand and became almost invisible.

The device began to shudder, and as Grace placed the thin plate in her pocket, the stealth device melted down and almost completely disintegrated, leaving practically nothing but dust on the floor.

Looking back around, everyone appeared to be recovering from the mini-disaster Grace had initiated. Again, she didn't notice the detective across the room, standing in the shadows. He had not taken his eyes from Grace and continued to watch her as she moved back toward the others.

"Oh ... I am soooo sorry. Please, let me help you!" She picked up a cloth napkin and attempted to help a man get food off his uniform.

The man glanced at her. "No, no. Just leave me alone. I'll get it."

Grace began picking up dishes and continued to apologize. She then noticed the commissioner walk back to the stage. Curiously, he stood for a second, scanning the wall as if searching for something. He then glanced back, and without noticing Grace, he stepped back to the podium.

After a few more words from the commissioner, the meeting was wrapped up hastily as most were covered with food or drink. Everyone was instructed to meet in Washington, DC.

Grace caught a short ride to the closest military installation. She then acquired transit to her home in Las Vegas.

CHAPTER THREE:

PIRATES COVE

It was 8:30pm when Grace wearily stepped into an elevator of her apartment building and pushed the button to the top floor.

Once the doors opened, Grace moved from the elevator and down an unfinished hallway. There was only one apartment at the end, and the walls were rough wood sheets that had yet to be painted. Unlocking the special order, "trans-view, security door," she stepped inside.

Once in her apartment, she tossed her small bag onto a plush couch. Then, she pulled off her long jacket as well as her holstered weapons and draped them across a chair. She then walked through her bedroom and on through another door that led to the other part of her dwelling.

There was a brisk breeze as she opened the door. The apartment was only half completed. One entire wall was unconstructed, and there were exposed steel beams as well as a large hoop used for construction that hung from a heavy chain.

The lights of Las Vegas glowed all around. A strong breeze

brushed her hair back. She gazed down twenty stories below and listened to the sounds of the city. Then, she jumped the two feet out and onto the construction hoop. It swung about as she got a better hold and then slipped inside. Sitting high above the streets below, she swung gently back and forth for about twenty minutes. Then, she turned her head after faintly hearing her doorbell ring.

Pulling herself up, then swinging a bit, she jumped back to the floor of her unfinished apartment. She moved through her bedroom and on to the front door.

Pressing a button beside the entryway, the door became transparent. Standing outside in the hall was a man in his mid-forties. He wore clean, pressed dress clothes. His dark-brown hair was tinted with gray, as was his thin mustache.

Grace pushed the button again, and the door darkened. She reached the knob and opened the door.

"Hello, Grace."

"Hello … Doctor Reese. Won't you come in?" She then turned and moved back to the large living area.

Once inside, Grace motioned to the couch. The doctor moved her bag over and sat down.

"Doctor Reese, again? We talked about this if you recall."

She sat down in a plush chair across from him.

"Yeah, fine, 'Father.'" She crossed her legs and then continued. "So, what brings you here?"

"Well, I just worry about you. I heard another mission has developed."

She studied him carefully. Then, she stood up and walked over to a beverage dispersal unit attached to the wall.

"How about a good stiff drink?" she asked and then pulled a large glass from a holder beside the dispersal unit.

"No, thanks. And I wish you wouldn't drink so much." He paused as she pushed several buttons on a selection screen. The unit quickly poured her a large, mixed drink.

He continued, "And, why must you spend so much time in the ghetto districts?"

Turning back around, she downed half the drink in what looked to be one swallow. She then caught her breath.

"Have you been spying on me, or is it your 'well-informed contacts,' again?"

Doctor Reese frowned. He then shifted his position on the couch.

Grace expelled a breath, walked over and sat the glass on a small table beside the chair.

"I've been up for almost forty-eight hours straight. I need a shower. If you change your mind about a drink, make yourself at home."

She then walked toward her bathroom, which did not have a door on it. Doctor Reese glanced over as she unzipped her outfit and began to take it off. He quickly turned away and waited for her to finish the shower.

Ten minutes later, she walked from the bathroom wearing a barely-there sleeping outfit with a sheer robe over it.

Doctor Reese expressed discomfort as she entered the room. She took her drink and sat down.

"So, did you just come here to express your concern for me?"

43

"Well, I suppose I missed you and just wanted to assure myself that you're okay. If I waited for you to visit me, I might never see you."

She smiled and downed another large portion of her drink.

"Is that what you want … Brad? You want me to visit you?"

"Grace, why must you torment me?"

"I'm tormenting you…? You come here and tell me that you're concerned about me. That you miss me. Tell me, is it the same concern you felt about my … mother?"

Doctor Reese winced. He looked down at the floor.

After finishing her drink, she set the glass back down on the table and stared at Doctor Reese. He looked up at her.

"Tell me about her … 'Father.'"

"I've already told you about her many times. You know very well, you're just like her."

"No, I don't want that. I want you to tell me about her again because I was never able to sit with her and have a conversation like you and I are having. I was never able to ask her about childhood memories or little things that might fill the emptiness."

He examined her briefly. "You've drunk too much, Grace."

"NO!" she shouted. "I've not drunk enough!" She stood up and, taking her glass, went to refill it. Afterward, he watched as she downed half of the drink and then sat down again.

"Tell me about her!"

His head lowered a little. "She was a special operations captain and a hero. She won the distinguished service medal during the death cult uprisings. She earned the medal of honor during the Caliden Conflict. She won many other honors and medals. She was the bravest person I've ever known." He again looked up at her. "I've told you all of this before, Grace. What's the point?"

She examined him with anger in her eyes. Finally, she responded.

"The point is, she died. She was killed in action. She made a mistake, and she was killed."

He expelled a long breath. "You're not her. You don't have to be her, Grace. You're better than she was."

She grunted and looked away.

"I'm better than she was? A distinguished hero with years of experience, you really think I'm better than she was. You really think I won't make a mistake? If you really believed that, Brad, this would be a much different conversation. You and I both know that."

She then downed the last of her drink.

Silence held the room for several long seconds. Then, Doctor Reese said softly, "You don't have to follow in her footsteps. Some things never change, and some things always change. But you don't know that her destiny and yours will be the same. You can change yours. You can live."

She looked at him. She was obviously exhausted, and the drinks were starting to affect her.

With her head bobbling slightly, she asked, "What did she fight for? What am I fighting for?"

Doctor Reese watched her as she appeared to be falling asleep. He replied, "She fought for everything in this world

45

that is good. And if she and others like her did not fight for these things, there would eventually be nothing good left to fight for."

Grace stared at him with glazed eyes. She mumbled.

"Yeah...well, medals and honor don't pay the bills."

Her head slowly lowered, and she fell asleep.

Doctor Reese walked over and picked her up. Then, he carried her to the bedroom. He placed her in bed and covered her up. After gently brushing her hair back, he leaned over and kissed her on the side of the head. Then, he quietly left her apartment.

The following morning, Grace woke to a throbbing headache. She took some meds, cleaned up, dressed, packed a few things and was soon headed out the door.

She boarded a military flight to Washington D.C., and after a tedious drive through the capital in a rented hovercar, she arrived at the designated assembly building. Walking in, she saw the group from the meeting in Vancouver were now gearing up for the mission.

Strolling over to Captain Bradford, she noticed he frowned as she approached him.

"Lieutenant Wolfe, I was hoping that little disaster in the meeting had prompted your exclusion from this mission."

Grace smiled. "Captain, you can't be serious. Look at all these drab and dreary army types. And who wears an outfit like that anymore?" She pointed to a man dressed in a clean-cut business suit. "That is sooo boring. You really need someone like me to liven up this little get-together."

Captain Bradford appeared to be barely containing himself. He almost grunted while expelling a breath of frustration.

"Lieutenant, this is not a 'get-together.' It is the launch point for a highly classified and dangerous mission."

Grace appeared not to hear the captain. She looked over his shoulder to one of the female members tying her hair back into a ponytail.

"I really like the color of her hair. Do you like that color, captain? I think I'll change my hair color after this mission thingy is over."

As Captain Bradford turned a light shade of red and looked to be on the verge of yelling at Grace, the commissioner walked up with a large man in combat gear. He wore body armor and carried a short automatic laser rifle.

"Captain Bradford, I would like Captain Evans to team with the lieutenant here."

Captain Evans expressed shock. "Are you joking, sir? You want me to team up with … clown girl?"

Captain Bradford also expressed surprise. "Commissioner, with all due respect, Captain Evans is one of the best commandos in our group. Why would you want to team him with …"? He turned to Grace, who simply smiled and observed the conversation as if clueless. Captain Bradford continued, "with the lieutenant."

The commissioner replied quickly. "Captain, I understand your concern. I would just like to avoid any casualties in the first hours of the operation. I believe, being teamed with Captain Evans, there could be a little more balance."

Both Captain Bradford and Captain Evans appeared to consider the situation. Then, Captain Bradford said, "Yes, I see what you mean. Perhaps that would help avoid a mess straight out of the gate."

With a chipper voice, Grace said, "Yes, I would love to team up with the captain here. Don't worry, captain. I'll watch out for you. We don't want you getting killed or anything right off the bat."

Captain Evans sneered at her. Captain Bradford spoke up with a stern voice. "Lieutenant Wolfe, you will follow Captain Evans' orders without question. He is the ranking officer, and if you do not follow his orders, I'll have you drummed out of the service." He glanced at the other two men and then mumbled under his breath, "I can't understand how that hasn't happened already."

The commissioner nodded. "Thank you, captain." He then walked away.

Captain Bradford looked at Grace and then to Captain Evans. "Well, just do the best you can, captain. I would suggest you keep her somewhere out of your way. Maybe she can fetch your coffee or something." He then walked away, as well.

Grace smiled and put out her hand to shake. "Well then, it seems we're teammates."

The captain looked at her hand but didn't shake it. He looked Grace over. "Is that what you plan on wearing? Do you have any body armor or weapons?"

Grace looked down at her sleek black outfit. "This is what I always wear. I love the way it fits … don't you?" She smiled coyly and then continued before the captain could comment.

"Oh, and I have two of these really nice guns." She pulled one side of her black trench coat back to reveal an automatic laser pistol strapped to her leg.

Captain Evans shook his head with a look of bewilderment. "Let's go then. It's your funeral."

As Captain Evans made his way to an information point, Grace followed behind.

Reaching a long desk, Captain Evans spoke to a woman sitting behind a holographic screen that displayed information.

"Captain Evans and …" He glanced back at Grace, "and, lieutenant something or other," he said, pointing to Grace.

Grace leaned toward the woman, "Lieutenant Wolfe."

The woman began entering information.

"You are to be briefed in room 7J. It's all the way down the hall and on the right. You may need to wait a few minutes if there's another team in the room."

The captain nodded and began walking down the hallway with Grace following behind.

Once the two were in the room, an officer came in and began the briefing.

"We have a lead for you two to follow up on concerning a potential link to a Fellirex smuggling point. It's located in a somewhat vacant area of the entertainment district of South, Pittsburg. You should be very careful. This is not considered as dangerous as the ghetto districts, but not by much. The location will be loaded into your communication devices."

The officer then handed each one a small cylindrical comm. device.

"These are your mission-issued communication devices. They should be kept with you at all times."

After additional information was relayed, he dismissed the two, and they returned to the main staging area.

Soon after this, they were led to a large bay that held helio-craft. They were directed to one, and as they boarded, Grace noticed a small armored hover vehicle loaded in the back. On the sides were "Trade Commission Authority" signs.

Moving up to the cockpit of the helio-craft, she turned to Captain Evans. "I'll drive. I'm an excellent driver!"

He took her arm and gently pulled her away from the pilot seat.

"Just go back there and sit down." He then sat and started the craft's engines. The hum of the jets grew in intensity as they warmed up. Ten minutes later, they were flying out of a large open doorway and climbing into the air.

After thirty minutes or so, Grace stuck her head inside the cockpit, "Do I get a turn to drive, or am I just supposed to sit back here the whole time?"

Captain Evans glanced back. "It'll take a while to get there. You may as well get comfortable."

An hour later, the craft landed. Captain Evans stood and walked back to the rear area. He found Grace sprawled out on the small bench seat, fast asleep.

Tapping her leg, she blinked and looked up at him, squinting.

"I didn't expect you to get that comfortable. Are you ready, or would you like to stay here and sleep?"

Sitting up, she rubbed the side of her face and then attempted to straighten her hair.

"Uhm, no. I want to go with you. We're going to an entertainment district, right? I sure hope there's a decent casino."

The captain shook his head in disbelief.

"Lieutenant, how on earth have you managed to survive with such a minuscule adroitness?"

Still adjusting her hair, Grace looked up and stared at him with dismay. Then, her head slowly drifted down until she was looking at her chest. Turning her attention back to the captain, she replied with a bit of defiance in her voice, "I'll have you know, captain, I'm a size thirty-six, which is considered above average, by the way!"

He closed his eyes and rubbed his forehead as Grace stood up. He then turned and began to unfasten the small armored vehicle. A few minutes later, both were in, and Captain Evans maneuvered it down a ramp and off the helio-craft.

From their location at a Trade Commission property in the upper-level business district, they moved to a lower-level entry point. As they descended several stories into the darker areas of the old city, Captain Evans glanced over to Grace. She was pulling her hair back and tying it into a ponytail.

The lightly armored hovercraft sped silently along the dusty and weather-worn streets. He glanced at Grace again, and she held her communication device up, using it as a mirror. As the passing streetlights lit up the interior, she appeared to be primping and examined her face as if checking for any blemishes. The captain shook his head again and returned his attention to the developing ghetto-like environment.

The buildings increasingly became dated in this area, and many were vacant. Fires burned in old barrels, and residents often huddled in groups around them, drinking and smoking. They heard loud music that faded as they sped past the gatherings. A gunshot sounded off in one building as they moved by quickly.

As the vehicle zipped silently past, people would occasionally yell out. Often, they would yell obscenities, but some would call out as if they admired the armored car flying by them.

After fifteen minutes of traveling through the aged district, the two arrived at a long street with numerous entertainment establishments. Long outdated LED signs flashed images of scantily clad women or gambling machines. As the captain and Grace climbed out of the vehicle, several men approached. They were obviously intoxicated or on some type of drug-induced high.

"Hey," one of them said to the captain. "I like your ride. You ain't from around here, are you?"

Grace examined the two men as the captain reached in and pulled his short laser rifle out. The men stepped back, and one said, "Whoooaaa, you got some jacked firepower there, amigo!"

As they stepped away from the vehicle, the captain touched a button on his wrist band. A loud and menacing voice said, "Warning, this property protected by THOR!" A large holographic hammer immediately swung out and around the vehicle. The two men stepped back even farther and then walked away, talking among themselves.

"It should be down here a block or so," the captain said as he led the way. "It's been identified as an old nightclub called 'Pirates Cove.'"

"Pirates Cove? Really? It sounds like one of those swanky, twentieth-century nostalgia joints." She then walked quickly to catch up to the captain, who paid no attention to her.

The two moved past rundown and vacant buildings, and then they passed an entertainment facility that was still open for business. The businesses that were open would often have women in risqué attire standing around the entrance as well as men offering drugs for sale. Grace noticed most of the men selling drugs were offering Fellirex.

As they approached a dilapidated building with a sign indicating it to be the Pirates Cove, Captain Evans readied his rifle and investigated a dirty window.

"It looks deserted. Perhaps the information was inaccurate."

Grace moved to the window and glanced in.

"Or, it may be a trap. I should go in first to make sure it's safe." She then pulled the automatic weapon from her right leg holster.

The captain stifled a laugh.

"Lieutenant—and I use that term lightly—I recently returned from a six-month Siberian training exercise. Believe me, I'll know a trap when I see one."

Grace's face became stretched for an instant, but before the captain noticed, her expression quickly turned to a quirky grin.

"Yeah, well … I recently returned from a two-week vacation in Hawaii, but that doesn't mean I would know a pineapple if I was to see one!"

He stared at her for several seconds with an odd expression, then checked his laser rifle one last time.

"No, you stay out here and … watch for trouble. I'll go in and check it out."

"Captain, if you'll not allow me to go in first, I would suggest we go in together."

As the captain powered up his laser rifle, he pushed open the front door with his foot.

"That's an order, lieutenant. This is likely a dead-end, but if it's not, I am perfectly capable of dealing with it myself."

Grace's eyebrows raised a bit, and she smiled slightly. "Fine, but don't say I didn't warn you." As soon as the captain moved toward the door, her smile fell flat.

Stepping into the large entrance, the captain glanced around a short hallway. This appeared to be where admission was paid at one time. Now, it was vacant, and paint peeled from the walls.

What the captain failed to notice was a small protrusion in a corner of the ceiling. As the captain investigated the entrance, a tiny camera scanned his face and identified him as being on the Fellirex case.

Stepping to the side, Grace examined the hallway from an angle rather than in front of the entrance.

Captain Evans moved down the hallway and then opened one of the double doors at the end. After looking in briefly, he moved into the nightclub.

Grace remained beside the entrance for a few seconds. Then, all hell seemed to break loose inside the building. Gunfire and laser weapons erupted into a crescendo of what could only be a firefight. Then, after a moment of chaos, all became quiet.

Still holding her weapon, she edged up to the entrance, crouched down and pushed a button on her laser pistol. A small screen from the side engaged and flipped over at an angle. She moved the end of the pistol to the front of the doorway, and the screen displayed the interior of the hallway. A small target lit up, revealing the almost invisible security camera mounted into the ceiling and toward the upper corner.

Pulling the trigger, she fired her pistol, and the camera was blown from its location. Retracting the screen back into her pistol, she stood and carefully moved into the hallway.

Moving up to the double doors, she crouched down to the side of one. Holding her laser pistol in the right hand, she used her left hand to push one of the doors open.

Immediately, bullets and laser fire erupted. Splinters from the doors rained down on Grace and all around her. She lowered herself a bit more and covered her head as the doors beside her disintegrated from the firepower.

Seconds later, the firing stopped, and all became quiet. Grace remained where she was. One of the shattered doors beside her fell from its hinges and landed on the floor with a thud.

Smoke and dust drifted inside the small hallway. Grace touched a button on her pistol, and the screen extended and turned to where she could view it. She then carefully moved the tip of her pistol to the edge of the doorway. On the small screen, she saw two armed men looking toward the doorway. Moving it slightly, she noticed another in the corner. Behind the two men were several automatic turret weapons that were extended from wall-mounted locations.

Moving the pistol carefully, she could see several bodies around the floor. She then spotted the leg of someone lying on the floor behind a bar area. On closer examination, she determined it to be Captain Evans' boot. Then, moving the pistol to the far side of the room, she spotted another armed man.

Pulling the pistol back, she touched the button, and the screen retracted to a flush position on the side of the weapon.

Reaching into a small pocket inside her jacket, Grace pulled out several items the size of marbles. She pressed on and then rolled one into the room, then, she pressed another and rolled it into the room. Almost immediately, the two items popped, and smoke began to fill the space.

Still crouching, Grace pulled the pistol from her other holster. Holding her two weapons in a ready position, she leaned over and rolled into the building. She stood up quickly and shot down the two men.

The automatic gun turrets began to fire just as Grace fell and rolled. Bullets ripped tables apart, and fragments flew all around her. She continued to roll until she reached a large pool table.

The turrets stopped firing. She touched a button on one pistol and then the other, making the small screens come out again. The one in her right hand came out on the left side, and on the pistol in her left hand, the screen came out on the right side.

The man in the corner yelled out.

"You're going to die! Give up now, and we'll let you live!"

Grace moved to the right side of the pool table. She moved her pistol around to where she could see the gun turret in her small screen. Lining it up in the sights, she fired. The blast knocked it out, but the other turret began to fire. Again, dust, splinters and bits of the pool table flew everywhere.

Grace held her head down and stayed still. The automatic gun turret stopped firing. Smoke and dust filled the air. One of the men coughed, and Grace noted the location. She then rolled to the left end of the table, and using the laser pistol in her left hand, spotted the remaining turret. She lined it up, shot and knocked it out of service.

Now, the two men began to fire at the pool table. Grace pushed the two buttons, and the small screens retracted. She rolled to her right and got herself into a crouching position.

The firing stopped, and she stood up. Immediately, Grace spotted and shot down one of the two men. She then dropped to the floor as bullets came from a corner area.

Grace crawled a few feet and then, rolling behind an overturned table, she aimed her pistol around the edge of the table and toward the direction where the shots emanated. Blasting the area with laser fire, the room became quiet.

Edging to the side of the table, Grace noticed the remaining man lying in the corner. She had hit him several times with laser fire.

She slowly stood and scanned the building for any remaining threats.

Moving cautiously to where Captain Evans laid, she holstered one of her pistols, reaching down and checked for a pulse. Finding he was still alive, she searched his uniform until locating five insta-medic, hypodermic shot pods. Pulling one from the pack, she quickly injected him with the lifesaving formula. She then placed the empty insta-medic shot in his open hand.

Standing back up, she moved across the large room that had once been a nightclub. Now, tables and chairs were strewn about, and a haze of smoke and dust permeated the air.

Stepping around several dead men, she approached the man in the corner. He was still alive, and from his appearance and dress, it seemed he was likely the leader. His right arm was blown off and lay a foot from him. His midsection was in pieces and almost disconnected from his upper body.

He looked up to her, his breathing labored.

Grace crouched down and began searching his pockets.

"Get the hell away from me, bitch!"

She smiled slightly and continued searching his pockets until she found his communication device. She examined the rolled-up tube.

The man continued in his labored breathing, then coughed

a couple times. It was apparent the pain was becoming excruciating. He groaned in agony as he watched Grace.

She turned and, reaching down, felt the dismembered hand and arm. It was still warm. Grace sat her laser pistol down, and taking the man's finger and thumb, placed them on the ends of the tube. The device unlocked and unrolled.

The leader's face became stretched with anger.

"You're a damn bitch! You're a gawd damn bitch, you hear me!"

Grace looked at him.

"Now, now, is that the way your mother taught you to talk?"

"Screw you, bitch!"

She picked up her pistol and holstered it as she stood, then began examining the open device but glanced around again to be sure she was safe.

Looking over to the dying man, she replied.

"Under different circumstances, I might find that flattering, but you're really not my type." She then examined his obliterated groin area. "And, I honestly don't believe you have the equipment left for such a thing."

He growled as she wandered over to a desk by the wall and a few feet from the wrecked turret. On the desk, she noticed a notebook-sized processing device.

Strolling over to it, she realized it was still functional but locked.

She stepped back over to the leader.

"What's the password for that notebook?"

He groaned in agony and then spit at her, but it fell short.

"You stupid bitch! Why do you think I would tell you that?"

She looked him over.

"Well, judging from your condition, I believe you will live another five to ten minutes. You're too far gone for an insta-medic. And help will not arrive in time. Your pain, however, will continue to increase a hundredfold as each minute passes, and each minute will feel like an hour."

His eyes belayed that he could barely comprehend his pain being more than it was at the time. She continued.

"Now, as it happens, I have a level-ten pain inhibitor with me. Giving me the password won't matter to you soon. So, why not make your last minutes peaceful?"

He groaned in agony as he considered this. His eyes squinted, and he trembled for several seconds.

"All right, all right! Give me the pain inhibitor, and I'll give you the password!"

She reached into her jacket and pulled out a small black case. Opening it, she scanned over an assortment of colored hypodermic pods. She ran her finger over a blue one, then a red one and a purple one. She stopped and glanced at the man. Then, she moved her finger to a yellow pod. Pulling it out, she removed the cap, which exposed the needle end and then tossed it down to the man.

As he used his remaining hand to grapple with the small pod, she asked.

"Password, please?"

He looked up.

"Greenland465."

She walked over to the notebook.

After struggling several seconds, the man was able to stick the needle into his side, and the pod automatically injected the contents into his body. He expelled a breath of relief as the injection took effect.

Meanwhile, Grace typed in the password he had given her. The screen displayed the password to be invalid. She walked back over to the man, who now sat calmly and seemed to have no more pain.

"It seems the password you gave me is invalid."

He looked up at her with glazed eyes, then smiled.

"You are a damn stupid ass bitch, aren't you? Did you really think I would give you the password?"

He laughed smugly.

Grace stared down at him with a stern expression.

"No, not actually. That's why I didn't really give you a level-ten pain inhibitor."

His expression immediately changed to surprise.

"What I gave you was Belvan truth serum. Incidentally, it does have a high pain-inhibiting side effect. It's also very rare and quite expensive, so let's not waste it. Now, what is the real password?"

The man became stern. He seemed to be resisting but blurted out, "Iceland654."

"Good, now don't you die on me, yet." She smiled, winked and walked over to the notebook. Typing in the new password, it immediately unlocked the device.

Taking the man's comm. device, which she had quickly placed in an unlocked state, she laid it on the notebook and started downloading the data. As the light flashed green, indicating a transfer, she walked back over to the man.

"Well, what else do you have for me, sparky?"

The man appeared to be dying now. His head bobbled a little.

"I don't know much; he keeps everything secret."

Grace knelt to the man as his voice was growing weak.

"Who keeps everything secret?"

"I only know him as 'Shadow-man.' He's the leader. He makes all the calls."

"Who do you report to?"

"My connection is someone with the code name 'Minotaur.'"

His head began to slump over.

"What else?"

"Diamonds," he blurted out.

"Diamonds? How many? Where?"

"Three million dollars' worth—all in natural, rough state."

"WHERE?" she shouted.

The man was almost dead. She grabbed his hair and lifted his head up.

"WHERE ARE THE DIAMONDS?"

He mumbled, "East Atlanta Sky Port, bay 6-B."

The man then died. She let his head drop and stood up.

The man's comm. device bleeped, indicating the data transfer to be complete. She walked over and put it in her pocket.

Grace then put the notebook back into a locked state, pulled her laser pistol out, stepped back a few feet and blasted the device, which flew off the desk and hit the wall.

She then searched her pockets until she located the comm. device that she was issued by the Trade Commission and, after looking around, walked over and dropped it into a pocket of the shattered pool table. She then moved over to a chair and sat down.

Forty minutes later, as the smoke and dust settled, soldiers entered the building with weapons drawn. As they moved around the room, systematically ensuring there were no threats, Grace glanced up from her efforts on the man's communication device.

One of the soldiers lowered his weapon and spoke into the device attached to his helmet. "Area secure, sir."

Directly after this, Captain Bradford walked in. Following him were several medics who rushed over to Captain Evans as soon as they spotted him. Captain Bradford looked at Grace sitting in a chair with her legs propped up on a table. He then spoke to one of the medics as they began to work on Captain Evans.

Grace casually glanced up again and observed the new developments as more soldiers entered and began investigating the battle scene and backrooms of the old nightclub. Captain Bradford moved over to Grace and glanced down at her with a frown. He looked around the building and expelled another breath of frustration.

"Unbelievable," he said and then looked back to Grace, who had tilted her head to observe him.

Dropping her legs from the table and sitting up, she looked around the building as the captain had done, then replied.

"I agree, captain. Who in their right mind would put the bar over there?" She pointed at the extensive bar along the wall. "With the stage over there." She pointed to the stage and continued. "Whoever designed this place knew nothing about entertainment. Everyone at the bar would need to twist around or practically get whiplash to watch the stage show. It's unbelievable!"

The captain appeared lost for words. His lips tightened, seeming to struggle to keep from saying something. Grace smiled, crossed her legs and went back to work on the communication device, clicking her nails several times with her free hand.

"Lieutenant Wolfe, we're here because Captain Evans' bio-detection device indicated he was severely injured."

Grace looked up from her efforts on the device. "You mean he's still alive?"

Captain Bradford seemed ready to explode. He took in another long breath and, appearing to regain his composure, continued.

"Apparently, he was able to administer an insta-medic pod before losing consciousness. Lieutenant, could you possibly clue me in on what happened here?"

Grace sat up a little more and said, "Certainly, captain. We arrived out front, and I asked Captain Evans if he wanted me to check things out first. But he insisted … Well, he ordered me to stay outside. I was a little concerned about it being a trap, but he said he could take care of himself. So, anyway, he came in, and there was a bunch of shooting and stuff! Well, it got quiet, and I felt I should check on the captain, and here I am! Then, you guys showed up. And I'm glad you did. It was getting very boring here, and in case you haven't noticed, it's … well, very dirty, as well as all the blood and body parts." She grimaced and looked at one of the dead men on the floor across the room.

Captain Bradford frowned again, took in a deep breath and glanced over to Captain Evans being moved out of the building on a hover-gurney.

"Go back to headquarters with the medics and Captain Evans. I'll have someone retrieve your mobile equipment, and I'll deal with you tomorrow when I get some time. Understand lieutenant?"

Grace smiled and stood up.

"Thank you, captain. It will certainly be nice to get away from this dive."

She then followed the medics to the transport vehicle and was soon headed back to headquarters.

CHAPTER FOUR:

HARD ROCKS

After a ninety-minute flight, Grace arrived at the mission HQ around 1:00pm. She stepped off the military helio-craft as medics rushed Captain Evans past her on the hover-gurney. From the mission HQ, she acquired a taxi to the ghetto district of Washington DC.

After paying the taxi driver, she entered a somewhat rundown techno shop that had classic "Mind-Bender" tunes playing in the background and smelled of weathered plastic.

Several men sat around in the dim light. As she passed by shelves of used devices and equipment, Grace approached a young man behind the front counter. He had a wiry build, dark hair and wore thick, power specs that emitted a slight cream-colored glow.

"FROG! You and me in the backroom … alone, NOW!"

The man looked up from his work on a small device.

"Grace, sweetheart! Where you been, love? I've been missing you like crazy!"

He smiled apprehensively as he examined her through the heavily framed power specs.

She walked up to the counter as the other men studied her with desire.

"Have you been cheating on me?"

"No, no … never, sweetheart. You're the only girl for me!"

"Let's go to the backroom, lover. I'll know right away if you've been playing around."

The men chuckled as Frog moved around the counter.

"Come on, guys. I need to close shop for a while. You know, take care of some important business."

The men grumbled but stood and somewhat reluctantly left the shop. Frog locked the door behind the last one. Turning to Grace, he smiled.

"You're priceless. Sweetheart, those guys, and every guy in the neighborhood for that matter, envy me!"

Grace sat on a stool in front of the counter.

"Well, I don't mind being your imaginary lover as long as you keep up your end of the bargain."

Frog moved back around the counter. He reached under it and brought out a bottle of liquid that was so black it almost looked like a bottle of tar or very strong coffee.

"Yeah, sure, Grace! Have I ever disappointed you?" He then pulled out two small glasses.

"No, but I've got a real challenge for you this time, so you'd better put your big-boy pants on."

As he poured the two glasses full, he expressed interest. Then, with both filled, he lifted the bottle for her to view.

"Kelluargan friczen … the real stuff."

She smiled slightly and took the drink. Holding it up in the dim light, she appeared to be checking for quality. Then, after taking a sip, she pulled a device from her pocket and sat it on the counter."

Frog also took a drink and then stared at the device for several seconds, seeming to have difficulty believing his poor eyesight.

"Wow, a Hacker 5000! These little gems are hard to find."

"Yeah, well, I need you to hop that little gem up. I need the platinum upgrade, and I need it by tomorrow, before noon."

Frog appeared shocked.

"That's a tall order, love. It'll cost you!"

"That's not all."

She pulled an item from another pocket. She held up what appeared to be a dark, thin octagon and then moved to hand the item to Frog.

He held out his hand, and she laid the item in it. Looking into his hand, the small item seemed to disappear. He could only see his hand, as the piece had completely blended in with his flesh. He expressed shock and fear.

"Aghhh, what the hell?"

"That's what I need you to find out. I removed it from a larger device before it went into self-destruct mode."

He lifted the item and looked at the back side, which remained dark.

"This is some freakish tech, sweetheart. You're talking a lot of money to get any info on this … and keep it quiet, which I'm guessing you also want. I suppose you need it by tomorrow as well?"

Grace nodded.

"Well, for both," he briefly thought, "I'm guessing 75,000, for starters."

He then looked at her with a sly smile. "Or … one night with you should cover it all. Maybe even a little credit left over." He took another sip of his drink but kept his eyes on Grace.

She leaned over very close to him.

"Frog, darling, I admire your persistence and unbridled aspiration, but I doubt you would survive all night with me. Even if you did, I would only break your heart in the morning. Then, we wouldn't have this wonderful relationship we have now."

He moved closer to kiss her. She moved back to avoid it, making him frown.

"I would be willing to take my chances. You know, better to have loved and lost than to never have loved at all."

Taking a drink, she examined him over the rim of the glass. She then set it down on the counter and seemed to be considering his words. He continued.

"You know, Grace, you're the only woman that I believe I would sell my soul for."

Her head twisted a bit. She rubbed the side of her glass with her finger and studied the small amount of liquid left inside. She then lifted the glass, finished the drink and sat it on the counter close to the bottle.

"Do you believe we have a soul?"

He tipped his glass, finishing his drink, then poured both glasses full and sat the bottle down.

69

"I suppose so. It seems to me the soul is what makes us who we are. We can't see it, but we're born with it."

Looking up at him, she considered his words. He looked down and examined the odd octagonal plate again.

"So, if everyone is born with a soul, do you think there is only one soul per person?"

He looked up.

"What the hell are you getting at, love? I don't know. I suppose that's the way it works, one soul per person."

She lifted the glass and finished the drink in one swallow, then set the glass back on the table with a slight thud.

"Do you believe in heaven and hell?"

"I don't know, Grace. I suppose I do, in a way."

She stared out into space for several seconds.

"I wonder where you go when you die if you have no soul."

He examined her for several seconds, then tipped his glass up and took a sip.

"That's some deep shit, sweetheart. I know about tech, but I don't have a clue on that one."

She took in a long, slow breath, pulled her comm. device from her pocket, unrolled it and punched a few buttons on the screen. Lifting it up to him, he reluctantly reached into his pocket and pulled his device out. Then, after tapping several buttons, he waved it in front of hers.

"That's eighty-five thousand, lover. I need both by tomorrow, before noon. I also need the stealth piece to remain a secret and do not lose it!"

Frog glanced at the screen of his device as Grace turned to leave out the back door.

"Yeah, yeah ... anything for you, my love."

Later that evening, she stood at her hotel window and gazed out over DC.

She sipped a drink and then held it in both hands, rubbing the side gently. For half an hour, she stood gazing out over the city. She then moved over to the dispenser and poured another stiff drink. Finally, around midnight, she lay down and slept.

The following morning, right before noon, she walked into Frog's tech shop. Once again, there were men as well as several women hanging out. Some were looking over gadgets, and others were talking.

"Frog, my love, I need you alone. I can't wait any longer."

Expelling a long breath, he looked up and expressed exhaustion. "Grace, sweetheart ... you almost did me in yesterday. I don't think any man can handle more than seven times a day."

With this comment, the customers expressed shock, and several men groaned with envy.

Moving up very close to him, Grace replied, "You're not just any man, lover. And I know you're good for at least eight. So, don't put me off any longer."

Several of the female customers giggled, and at least one man grunted in disbelief. But all paid close attention to the conversation.

Frog gazed into Grace's eyes, seeming to want the charade to be real. Then, he exhaled slowly.

"All right, everyone, I need to close the shop for a while. You know, a man has to take care of his special girl."

Once everyone was ushered out, Grace sat on a stool, and Frog went to the other side of the counter. He pulled the Hacker 5000 out first.

"So, as it turns out, it's a good thing you gave me some extra money. Have you ever heard of Ghost 57?"

Grace shook her head, indicating she hadn't.

"Well, that doesn't surprise me, but in the underworld of tech, she's the best of the best. She was about to catch a hyper-jump to Ecuador when my contact offered the upgrade job. I told my contact that money was no object, so he negotiated with Ghost until he reached a deal of 65,000 dollars. But it's well worth every dollar. This little baby will do more than you could dream of doing with most federation hackers. And I wouldn't be caught with this if I were you. I don't know who you work for, love, and probably don't want to know. But this little hotrod could get you some serious time in a detention center."

Frog handed her the Hacker 5000. She looked it over as he pulled the small stealth plate out.

"Now, as for this little bugger, I would love to have gotten a look at the device you took it from. But I suspect that little look could cost me my life sooner or later, so I don't want to know any more than what I know now."

He examined the item closely and then handed it to Grace.

That is some Rocasion tech as far as my contacts can tell. The Rocas are deep into stealth and shape manipulation,

72

among other things. My sources 'think' that little item could reshape when it was connected to the device you said self-destructed. But, we all know, the Rocas were disenfranchised from the global trading agreement ten years ago. So, how does this Roca tech get here? Again, I don't really want to know, but I would speculate, the Rocas are up to something and knowing their nature, it is likely something no good. I would suggest you back out of whatever it is you're into as soon as possible."

Grace examined the thin plate. Then, she looked to Frog.

"Is that all you could get?"

He winced, and the power specs enhanced his eyes as they widened.

"Listen, sister, my sources were very nervous about even touching that thing. The Rocas play dirty if they play at all. As it was, I used the other twenty thousand and had to throw in ten thousand of my own just to get that."

She stuck the small plate into a breast pocket on her skintight suit, then looked out over Frog, as if in thought. Then she asked, "Do the Rocas deal in Fellirex?"

Frog shook his head, unsure. "I don't know. From what I understand, they deal with anything that will get them salt."

"Salt?"

"Well, it's only hearsay from shadow channels of the tech world, but the whole story about the Rocas stealing weapons and getting disenfranchised from the global trade union is said to have been a cover for the real crime that got them kicked out of the trade partnership. Word is, salt is like gold in their little corner of the galaxy. But they hid this fact from the Trade Commission and made indirect deals with several major suppliers. When the Trade Commission found out they were raking it in by trading for our salt in what amounted to a few dollars per pound and then sneaking it out classified as low-grade minerals, the Trade Commission kicked them out. Word is the Trade Commission wants to keep a lid on the salt information. They figure every two-bit criminal around would be trying to make deals with the Rocas if the information was public. I just think the Trade Commission wants to make all the money themselves ... if any of that is actually true."

Grace pulled her comm. device out and tapped several buttons on the display. She held it up. Frog lifted his up, and the transfer indicated fifty thousand dollars on his device.

"Thanks, lover."

Frog smiled as Grace stood up and started toward the back door.

"Grace!"

She turned back to him.

"Be careful. It may never be what I would like for it to be, but I don't want to lose what we've got."

She smiled. "I will. Don't worry, love. I'll be back to pester you again before you know it."

He nodded as she turned and left the shop.

Entering the busy mission HQ several hours later, Grace strolled over to a rest area and pulled out the small communication device she had taken from the leader at

Pirates Cove. She began to scour the information she had downloaded.

Twenty minutes later, Detective Vandenberg was walking past and noticed her sitting in the rest area. He watched her for a minute. The detective then started walking toward her but stopped halfway. He rubbed the back of his neck and glanced around nervously as uniformed personnel passed him by. A few seconds later, and seeming to regain his courage, he once again proceeded toward Grace.

As he stepped up to her, she appeared unaware of his approach. She held the comm. device in one hand, rapidly thumbing through the information and was clicking her nails together with the other.

He briefly stood in front of her as she busily scanned the small device in her hand.

"Uhmm," he cleared his throat, and Grace looked up at him.

"Uhhh, hello, Lieutenant Wolfe."

She examined him curiously.

"Hello. … Have we met?"

"Well, not really. I was at the commissioner's briefing in Vancouver. I actually arrived late."

"Oh, yes … I recall now. You're that inspector from Austria!"

Detective Vandenberg grimaced.

"Well, actually, I'm a detective, and I'm from the Antarctic Mining Colonies."

Grace smiled brightly.

"Oh, well, I was close then … Antarctica, Austria … you're all neighbors, right?"

Again, he expressed unease but pointed at the seat across from Grace.

"Do you mind if I sit?"

"No, please do … detective, uhm?"

"Vandenberg."

"Yes, that's right. Detective Vandenberg."

The detective sat down and, rather sheepishly studied Grace as she directed her attention back to the small communication device.

After observing her for a minute, he asked, "So you're a lieutenant. I wondered what branch of the military service you're in."

Looking up at him, she smiled again, then pressed the device on both ends causing it to roll up. She stuck the now small cylindrical item in her pocket, sat up, re-crossed her legs to the other side, then examined the detective several seconds before replying.

"I'm in Special Operations. It's a branch of the army."

The detective nodded and cleared his throat.

"It sounds very exciting. We don't get much excitement in the mining colonies. The only big crime I've solved was a murder case, but that seems to have made me the top detective in the colonies. I'm not sure I belong here with all the decorated heroes."

After studying him for a few more seconds, Grace replied, "Nonsense, detective. A hero is simply someone who does what must be done when it must be done and, by doing so, protects or saves those who are not able to act. It seems you're here now and willing to do what must be done. I doubt there's any difference between you and most of the others assigned to this case."

He smiled. "That's very kind of you to say."

Before the detective could continue, Captain Bradford approached the two. Detective Vandenberg stood up, but Grace remained sitting with her legs crossed. She leaned back in her chair to look up to him.

"Hello, captain."

"Hello, detective." He then looked down at Grace with anger-filled eyes. She turned her head slightly to acknowledge the captain but made no move otherwise.

"Just where the hell have you been, Lieutenant Wolfe?"

"I had some errands to take care of, captain. What can I do for you?"

He straightened up. His face seemed to swell a little.

"I'm relieving you from this assignment."

Detective Vandenberg expressed surprise, but Grace appeared unmoved.

"Really, and why is that?"

"Your teammate is seriously injured, and it will take time for him to recover. Therefore, I'm taking you off the case."

Grace smiled and almost replied, but Detective Vandenberg spoke up.

"Sir, I'll volunteer to work with the lieutenant."

Captain Bradford looked at him with disappointment. Grace also looked at the detective with a bit of wonder.

"Detective, you're assigned to duties in the rear, not field duty."

"Yes, sir, but I believe, as a detective, I qualify for field duty."

This seemed to frustrate the captain. He glanced down at Grace, who sat watching curiously. Finally, after a groan that almost sounded painful, he replied.

"No, I'm relieving Lieutenant Wolfe from this assignment." He turned to Grace. "You can gather your things, lieutenant. You're no longer on this mission."

Grace smiled with delight.

"That is wonderful, captain. I should be able to get a late appointment at the spa. I desperately need a good cleaning and such." She paused as if thinking of something and then continued.

"However, before I can leave, you will need to contact my commanding officer, General Sweetie, I mean, General Thomas, concerning the change of events. You know, all that military protocol and stuff." She again smiled brightly.

The captain rubbed his forehead but quickly responded, "If it gets you on the way to the spa, I'll gladly do that, lieutenant."

He turned and walked back toward the office area. Detective Vandenberg looked down at Grace.

"Well, I tried, lieutenant. I would have liked to work with you."

Grace studied the detective curiously. As he turned in preparation to leave, Grace asked, "Just what would possess you to want to work with me, detective?"

He turned back and, after seeming to consider the question, replied.

"Uhmm, well … I just feel there's more to you than meets the eye."

Grace smiled with glee and then chuckled.

"You can be certain of that."

He raised his hand, then rubbed it on his chest and fidgeted a bit.

"I didn't mean like… Well, I just meant … It's like uhm … I mean, you seem to have a multi-faceted personality. I've got a feeling there's more to you than most people see."

She continued to stare at him curiously and didn't respond, so he rubbed the side of his head and went on.

"And, I don't know if you've spent much time in a mining colony, but they're very uneventful in the area of excitement. When I was assigned this mission, I thought it would be something more than shuffling files. But so far, the only excitement I've witnessed is a minor spill at the water dispenser."

Grace's lips pressed together in a slight smile, seeming to imagine such a thing.

He nodded nervously, then continued.

"Well, I suppose it's neither here nor there now. I hope you make it to the spa on time."

Before he took a step, Grace responded.

"Detective Vandenberg. If you truly wish to work with me, I suggest you wait around for a few more minutes. However, I suspect you will question that decision before it's over with.

And, I should inform you that in the area of excitement, I've been known to … well, exceed expectations."

She paused for a second, then continued.

"Having said that, and if you're certain it's what you wish, I'm willing to be your teammate."

The detective appeared puzzled by this. His head twisted slightly, but he moved back to the chair and sat down. Grace watched him briefly, then pulled the small communication device out, opened it and again began to scan the information.

Five minutes later, Captain Bradford walked up to the two. Detective Vandenberg noticed he appeared pale as if he had seen something frightening.

Grace sat, scanning the comm. device with one hand and clicking her nails together with the other. Captain Bradford stood for several seconds. Grace didn't appear to notice he had approached, but the detective suspected she was ignoring him.

"Uhm," he cleared his throat, and Grace looked up to him. "Uhhm, well, after some discussion with General Thomas, I've decided to leave you on the case, lieutenant."

Grace sat up a little.

"Really? Now, that is interesting." She glanced across the room in thought. The detective watched as she then looked up to the captain again.

"Well, it's a good thing I waited to make an appointment. And, I'm not all that disappointed about it, as I've got a lead in the case that I was planning to follow up on."

"A lead?" the captain asked.

"Yes, you see, while I was sitting in the nightclub waiting for someone to arrive, I noticed several shipping boxes in the corner. They were from the East Atlanta Sky Port Company. Now, I suspect something is going on there that should be checked out."

Captain Bradford glanced over to the detective, seeming to want assurance that he was not the only one confused.

Grace stood up, stuck the comm. device in a pocket and continued, "And it's a good thing I'll be alone." She rather clumsily pulled her automatic weapon out and waved it around a bit, seeming to check its readiness.

As the captain ducked to avoid the front of the weapon, Grace said, "There may be some combat involved."

Then, with some effort, she re-holstered her weapon.

Captain Bradford grew even paler. He seemed a little ill as he looked at Detective Vandenberg again.

"Uhm, detective, could I have a word with you?"

The detective stood up. "Certainly, captain."

As they moved a few yards from Grace, she sat back down and again began examining the small communication device from the nightclub.

Once they were out of earshot, the captain leaned over to the detective.

"Listen, detective, I've decided to team you up with Lieutenant Wolfe." He glanced back to Grace and then continued. "Just follow her around and keep her out of trouble … and out of my hair. You got that, detective?"

"Yes, sir. I've got it. Thank you."

The captain started to walk back toward Grace but looked back at the detective. He grimaced a bit. "And don't let her kill anyone, including yourself."

This comment seemed to startle the detective, but he nodded.

Captain Bradford then moved back to Grace with the detective following.

"Lieutenant, I've decided to team up Detective Vandenberg with you. I would rather not send an operative out alone."

Grace again stood up.

"Well, are you sure about this, captain? It could be dangerous for him."

"Yes, well, I'm certain. I believe the detective is aware of the dangers involved in working with you. So ... uhm, go check your lead out, and please, let's not have any civilian casualties."

Grace appeared unsettled.

"Captain, if the general told you about that unfortunate incident in Columbia, you can rest assured it was not entirely my fault. I've also heard that little town is recovering quite well ... finally."

Seeming to turn another shade of pale, the captain asked, "Lieutenant, I'm assuming there is a reason I'm unaware of why General Thomas places such a high priority on your value as an operative. Could you please enlighten me on those qualifications?"

She perked up.

"Well, certainly, captain. As it happens, the general throws the most fantastic pool parties with lots of dignitaries and such that need to be impressed. And the general always wants me to be ready to attend and ... well, entertain and such. In fact, I never go anywhere without my bikini, just in case the general needs me to catch a flight and be present at one of his parties."

She reached into a pocket and produced a flat, round pouch about the size of a large coin.

"Would you like to see it?"

Captain Bradford examined the tiny pouch for several seconds then shook his head.

"No thanks, lieutenant, but that does explain a lot."

He then walked away, mumbling to himself.

Grace glanced at the detective, who also stared at the tiny pouch in her hand. He then looked up to her.

"Is that, uhhm ... is that really a swimming suit?"

She smiled and put it back into her pocket.

"I'm going to locate the motor pool. I suggest you wrap up any loose ends, get some rest and meet me back here around six tomorrow morning."

Detective Vandenberg smiled sheepishly, nodded and walked away.

The following morning, he returned bright and early to find Grace sitting in the same chair, again scanning the communication device. He also noticed she was dressed in what appeared to be the same outfit, though he suspected it was just an identical one.

"Good morning, lieutenant."

She stood up. "Good morning, detective. Are you ready?"

"Yes, I believe so."

She began walking, and he followed her.

Ten minutes later, they moved up to the front of the transportation motor-pool gate. A soldier examined them as they approached.

"Can I help you?" the soldier asked.

"Yes. I'm Lieutenant Wolfe, and this is Detective Vandenberg. We need a hovercar, something fast, like a Mach Seven—purple if you have it."

The soldier chuckled. "Well, we do have one Mach Seven, but you need to be a general or something close to it to requisition a ride like that. I've got some basic transportation you might qualify for."

Grace gave the soldier a frown. She then pulled her jacket back enough to reveal the small badge on her chest.

The soldier scanned the badge, and the holographic image of Grace appeared. The soldier looked over the credentials that floated under her picture. He then seemed a little embarrassed.

"I apologize, lieutenant. You're the first junior officer I've seen that has clearance for a Mach Seven. Let me get the order worked up, and you can get on your way."

After Grace signed the authorization, they were escorted to a corner of the motor pool where a jet-black Mach Seven sat.

"Black? Is this the only one you have? My outfit is black. Do you have a white one, at least?"

As Grace protested the color, and the soldier walked away,

detective Vandenberg admired the sleek performance hovercar.

"I like it. We don't have anything like this at the mining colonies."

Grace huffed a bit and opened the driver's side door. The detective opened his door, and the two were soon flying down the city streets toward a skyway entrance point.

"So, where are we off to?"

Grace glanced over to her passenger.

"Atlanta."

He looked at her, and his eyebrows raised a little.

"Do you really think a few boxes qualify as a lead?" he asked as they jetted upward and into the higher skyway traffic.

"Well, I do have a few additional clues. I really don't like working with a crowd around. If I told the captain everything I know, he would have a herd of people swarming around the area. I know how guys like him work. They always send in the armored destroyers when a few good foot soldiers are all that's needed."

As Grace maneuvered the vehicle along the mass of hover traffic, the detective grabbed the door. He leaned over and glanced at the speed display.

"Uhm, you do realize you're going two hundred and fifty miles per hour?"

Glancing down, she replied, "Oh, I thought I was going faster than that." She then sped up and again whizzed between several large transports.

"Well, are you aware the speed limit is two hundred ... And you do know these things have autopilot, right?"

"Are you frightened of my driving?"

"Oh, maybe not so much you're driving as anyone I'm riding with who is exceeding the speed limit by fifty or sixty miles per hour. We really don't have long, interstate skyways in the Antarctic. It's more like 'smoothly and safely,' down there."

Grace smiled but continued to speed along and pass vehicle after vehicle.

"So, it seems you don't really trust your superiors," he said, seeming to calm somewhat.

"In my line of work, no one is trusted. And to be fair, no one trusts me, so it all works out."

The detective nodded but seemed a bit unsure about her response.

After a quick stop for lunch, the two returned to their journey and were soon exiting the skyway and moving down into Atlanta. Twenty minutes later, Grace shut down the vehicle in the parking area of a major transport district.

Once out of the Mach Seven, and both doors were shut, Grace pushed a button on the vehicle's controller. A voice came from the hovercar.

"Warning, this property protected by ... COBRA!" A holographic cobra materialized over the car and raised its head as if about to strike. Then, the hologram disappeared as the two began walking away.

Detective Vandenberg moved swiftly to catch up to Grace. As they approached a gate with an "East Atlanta Sky Port

Company" sign, he noticed her reach into her jacket and pull out a pair of sunglasses.

Grace put the glasses on as they moved up to a guard shack. A large and well-armed security guard stepped out.

"Can I help you?"

"I need to talk with an associate in bay 6-B."

The guard eyed Grace up and down.

"Do you have clearance?"

"Well, do I need clearance?"

The detective stood behind Grace. He put his hand up to his forehead, seeming not to want to be in the situation.

"You'll need clearance to enter. This is private property."

Grace moaned in frustration.

"All right, here's the thing. My boss, Minotaur, was supposed to contact you and let you know we were on the way. You can either let us in now, or you can explain to my boss why you didn't let us take care of his business."

For several long seconds, the man just looked at Grace and then the detective. Finally, he motioned for them to pass.

Grace smiled and walked through the gate. A few feet past him, she reached up and touched the side of her sunglasses. A small screen displayed inside her glasses, and it presented the view from behind her. As she and the detective moved away, she watched the guard step inside the small shack, pick up a communication device and talk to someone.

"I sense a welcome party, detective."

"What?" he asked as they passed by large bay doors.

Grace pulled her glasses off and put them back in a jacket pocket. She turned to him and smiled but didn't offer a reply.

Detective Vandenberg's attention was quickly swayed by the massive transport craft he could see in open bay doors. These were craft that carried cargo around the world as well as into the spaceports that were dispersed close to the planet and some around the moon. Goods from the earth would be brought to these space stations, and goods from other planets would be loaded and brought back to earth.

"I used to dream of being a transport pilot," he said as they passed another open bay door.

Grace slowed and appeared to be searching for a certain bay. She glanced back as they stopped briefly in front of a sign with "5-B," displayed.

"So, what made you decide to be a detective instead?" Grace asked as she moved toward the next bay door, which was closed.

"I thought the criminal justice field would be a little more exciting. I suppose I was wrong about that."

They stepped in front of the smaller door beside the larger bay doors. Grace pulled a small hair tie from her jacket pocket. She quickly pulled her hair back and put it into a ponytail. Then, she pulled the two sides of her long jacket back and pinned them together behind her. This allowed for her two laser pistols to be easily accessed.

The detective watched this curiously. Grace glanced at him.

"Do you have a weapon, detective?"

His face twisted a bit, "A what?"

She pulled one of her pistols out and readied it.

"No? Well, perhaps one will turn up."

As she pushed a button to open the door, the detective asked again, "What?"

"Watch yourself," she said and stepped inside.

Immediately, gun and laser fire erupted in a sudden chaotic second. Detective Vandenberg stepped back, almost stumbling, and dropped to the ground as several shots glanced off the entrance.

He ducked and covered his head as more fire erupted.

There was a strong urge to check on the lieutenant, but he was too frightened to move.

After a minute of what sounded like pure unbridled hell, it became quiet. Still lying on the ground, the detective cautiously crawled over to the door and peeked in.

Grace stood with her back to a large cargo container. Beyond her, a massive cargo vessel sat in the bay. She held both laser pistols in a ready position. Around ten yards to Grace's front and to the rear of the cargo ship were four dead men, and toward a corner, one dead woman.

As he examined the battle area, a man moved from the far side of the large transport. As he moved forward with a rifle in hand, another man came from a door, also charging toward Grace.

Detective Vandenberg wanted to shout a warning to her. As the words struggled to come out, she turned and stepped out from her secure spot. Lowering her weapons as the two men took aim, she fired two shots almost simultaneously. Both men flew backward and onto the floor dead.

Scanning the area, Grace raised her weapons slightly but still held them in a ready position.

All was quiet again, and after several seconds, Detective Vandenberg stood and eased carefully into the bay.

As Grace glanced over to him, he stepped up to a dead man on the floor.

"Oh my God, lieutenant! I told Captain Bradford I wouldn't let you kill anyone! Damn! You just killed a bunch of people!"

Grace holstered her weapons.

"Why in the galaxy would you tell him such a thing, detective?"

He looked over to her, still displaying an ill expression on his face.

"Well, I suppose he asked me not to let you kill anyone, more than I told him I wouldn't let you. Damn, though, lieutenant! Why did you kill them?"

She began looking around but casually replied, "They're bad people, detective. They shot at me first."

"Yeah, but how do you know they're bad?"

"They've got guns."

"Lieutenant, almost everyone in this part of a city has a gun. Damn ... are you sure they're bad? I mean, you came down here to investigate boxes, right? Do you suppose they may have just thought you were an intruder?"

She appeared uninterested in the conversation and moved toward the entrance of the ship. Stepping onto the ramp of the large transport, she put her right hand on her holstered weapon and proceeded with caution up and into the vessel.

The detective moved toward the ramp. Stepping past another dead man a few feet from the entrance, he glanced down. "Crap, this is going to kill my resume," he mumbled to himself.

Following Grace, he moved down a narrow hall and then up steps. He found himself in the spacious cargo area of the transport ship. It was empty, and their steps echoed in the cavernous interior. They then moved up another long row of steps. By the time the two reached the cockpit, the detective was feeling winded.

Stepping inside the flight control center, he saw Grace examining the pilot's console. She then spotted a laser pistol laying to the side of a panel.

"Here you go, detective. This is a nice model. It has automatic if needed."

He took the weapon almost if she were handing him a snake. He examined it with a disgusted look.

"I uh, well, I really don't think I'll need this."

"Suit yourself, but I expect you'll be needing it before we're done."

"And, when do you suppose we'll be done?"

"That depends on where we end up next."

She pulled something from her jacket pocket and examining the device, she tapped a few buttons on the screen and sat it on the control console.

"Is that a Hacker?" the detective asked, turning and setting the laser pistol down behind him as if it were poison.

"Yes."

"Aren't they illegal?"

"Very."

Lights on the Hacker blinked, and a very slight humming emanated from the unit. Then, the control panel lit up.

Grace smiled as she picked the Hacker up and placed it back in her pocket.

"Wow, I didn't realize they could do something like that—and so fast."

Grace sat down in the pilot's seat and quickly began to move items around on the display. The ship began to vibrate as the engines started.

"Uhmm, just what is it we're doing?"

Without looking up from the display, she replied, "I'm activating the coordinates for this transport's regular run."

The doors slowly closed and began to seal. The detective looked around nervously as a "fasten seatbelts" sign lit up. He sat down in the copilot's seat and pulled the strap around him just as the ship began to lift out of the bay.

The massive cargo vessel hovered above the port facilities as the display indicated a pre-trip sequence taking place.

Grace scanned the console as the detective looked out the window and noticed other transport vessels arriving at the port and leaving it.

"So, just where are we headed?" he asked nervously, still observing the activity around the port.

"The stairway to hell! I've always wanted to go there, but I never thought I would go on a cargo transport."

As the huge ship began to move from the port and fall in line with others, Grace unbuckled her seatbelt and stood up.

"Stairway to hell? Can you be a bit more specific, lieutenant?"

She smiled. "I'm afraid not, detective. There are some things a woman feels she needs to keep close to her chest." She laid her hand over the top of her left breast. "This is one of those things."

For several seconds, they just looked at each other. Then, she continued, "The ship will autopilot itself to the destination. It is interesting to me that this vessel has security clearances that allow it to move through several continental areas without inspection. Don't you think that's curious, detective?"

He appeared in thought and then said, "I really wouldn't know since I'm not in the transport business."

"Well, I find it very interesting. I think it would take someone with very high credentials to get that type of clearance through the Trade Commission." She turned. "It'll take a while to reach our destination. I'm going to nose around for something to eat and then take a nap."

Unbuckling himself, he stood and followed Grace to the small crew kitchen. There, he sat at a table as Grace rummaged through the various food containers. She offered him an apple. He took a bite, watching her closely.

"So, do you kill people often in your line of work?" he finally asked.

After turning up a container of infused-seltzer and almost finishing it off in one drink, she pulled it down, wiped her mouth with the back of her hand and looked at the detective curiously.

He took another bite of the apple. The ship hummed around them. Grace flipped a chair around and straddled it.

She rested her arms on the back of the chair and, still holding her seltzer, studied him for several seconds.

"Do you have fond memories of your childhood, detective?"

He finished his bite and swallowed.

"Do you have a habit of answering a question with a question?"

She turned the seltzer up and finished the last of it. Then, she set the empty container on the table.

"I didn't answer your question at all. I chose to ask you a question of my own."

He looked at her with suspicion.

"Yes, I have fond memories of my childhood. My father is a miner. My mother is a computer technician for the mining company. The colonies are as deep as two hundred feet below the surface in some areas. I remember dreaming of going to a place where it was warm, and I could see the sky."

Grace examined his face as he spoke. He paused as she seemed to be captivated by his story.

"What about your mother and father? Were they nice to you as a child? Did they discipline you often? Did you have wonderful birthday parties?"

He looked at his half-eaten apple as if he wanted to take a bite rather than answer her questions, but he replied to her instead.

"Certainly, they're nice. They're like most parents. Weren't yours nice when you were a child?"

Grace stood up. "We were talking about your parents, not mine."

She walked over to a poster on the wall, indicating a safe trip was a successful trip. She studied it briefly.

"Do you believe in God, detective?"

He stopped chewing and looked at her, though all he could see was her back.

"Well, I find it hard to believe we could come from random chance. All the scientists ignore the impossible odds of living, thinking beings just springing up from dirt out of pure chance. I mean, to me, it would be like putting all the components of a cargo transport in a field and saying in a few million years the wind and rain would assemble it into a functioning ship."

She turned around, walked over and facing him, straddled the chair again.

"That is a very interesting way to put it. So, if there is a God, and each baby gets one soul, what happens to someone who didn't get a soul?"

He now examined her as if she were drunk.

"How could someone end up without a soul?"

She stared at him.

"Detective, I often wonder if I have a soul. And if I don't have a soul, does that mean I can do whatever I want? Or does it mean I'm destined for hell, no matter how good I am?"

His face twisted in confusion. He looked at the apple, seeming to still want to take a bite rather than continue the conversation, but he replied.

"You don't drink much, do you? This is the first time I've seen anyone get intoxicated off a single infused-seltzer."

Still seeming to be in thought and barely listening to his response, she stood up and moved toward the door.

"I'm going to take a nap." She disappeared down the narrow hall.

A moment later, Detective Vandenberg stood and glanced out the door. Seeing Grace was not close by, he pulled his communication device out. A few minutes later, and after several transfers, he was connected to Captain Bradford.

"What is it, detective?"

He again glanced out the door and then quickly moved back.

"Uhm, sir, you know what you said about trying to keep Lieutenant Wolfe from killing anyone? Well, I uhm, I wasn't able to keep her from doing that."

What could be described as a shriek was heard, and the detective placed his hand over the device to muffle it. A second later, the captain replied in a loud voice.

"What happened? Where are you? Where is she?"

The detective again held his hand slightly over the comm. device and glanced back out the door. After assuring himself that she was not around, he stepped back and replied.

"She's, well, I think she's taking a nap. We're on an empty cargo transport. She took over the controls, and we're in transit somewhere. We went to the East Atlanta Sky Port, and I followed her to bay 6-B. She, well, she opened the door, and there was a firefight. I'm afraid there are at least seven dead, sir."

"Aghhhh, I can't believe it! I don't know what General

Thomas was thinking." He paused for a second and continued. "I need you to apprehend Lieutenant Wolfe, detective."

"WHAT!" He then lowered his voice. "Sir, there's no way I can do that, and I'll not even try. I have not had enough training handling a weapon, and it's apparent she knows how to handle more than one at a time. I'm sorry, sir, but that is out of the question. I have no desire to commit suicide."

A groan emitted from the captain.

"Did you get a mission-issued comm. device before you left?"

"Uhm, no sir. I just have my personal communication device."

"Damn it! Damn it all!" Captain Bradford almost shouted.

"I can't put a trace on a private device. And we recently found Lieutenant Wolfe's device back at the nightclub where Captain Evans was injured. She probably lost it looking for a nail file or something. Where are you headed?"

"I'm not sure. She said the 'stairway to hell,' wherever that is."

"Damn it all. I don't need this right now. We're having a hell of a time with this mission as it is. I don't need to be dealing with Lieutenant Wolfe's nonsense." Again, he paused.

"You'll have to keep me informed, detective. I'll give you my personal number. Contact me night or day. I'll get an investigator over to the East Atlanta Sky Port and try to find out about the transport you're on. In the meantime, try to keep her from killing anyone else. And try to find out where you're headed or when you get there, let me know where you are. I'll send a squad to arrest Lieutenant Wolfe as soon as possible."

Detective Vandenberg winced a little but didn't reply.

"You get that, detective?"

"Uhm, yes, sir."

"Good. Keep me updated and try to keep her from doing any more damage."

The device went silent. He touched the screen, and it rolled up into a small cylinder. Placing it in his pocket, he peeked out the door once more. Then, he went back and found another apple. He sat back down at the small table and ate it.

Afterward, he went and found a bunk to lie down on. He took a nap for what he thought to be a few hours. After waking and finding the bathroom, he wandered around the vessel until he spotted Grace in what looked to be the ship captain's quarters.

He stood in the door as she was holding the Hacker up to a wall safe.

After several seconds, the Hacker flashed green, and she opened the safe door. Reaching in, she began pulling the contents out. Tossing papers and a few other items on a table, she then pulled out a bag. Turning around, she spotted the detective in the doorway.

"There you are detective. You're just in time!"

"Time for what?"

She opened the small bag, and stepping over to another table, poured out a pile of what looked to be rocks.

"What is it?" he asked.

"Raw diamonds! Several million dollars' worth." She smiled and raking the pile of raw diamonds back into her hand, began to pour them back into the small bag.

"What are you going to do with your share?"

His face twisted, almost as if in pain.

"My share? I don't have a share, lieutenant! Why on earth would you hack the captain's safe? You're a thief!"

She gazed over to him, still tying up the pouch. She appeared somewhat hurt or insulted.

"Detective, if we take something from a criminal, is it really stealing?"

Detective Vandenberg shook his head. He expelled a breath of frustration.

"Lieutenant, using some sort of warped philosophy to justify taking what's not yours does not make it right."

Grace stuffed the small bag into a pocket and walked out the door. The detective followed her. She went into the kitchen and over to the cooler, then pulled out another seltzer and opened it as the detective ran his hand through his hair in frustration. She took a large drink of the seltzer and then pulled the container down to study the man.

Turning to her and seeming to calm somewhat, he continued.

"Has it occurred to you that we're on a mission to stop the infiltration of Fellirex, and that so far, we've seen no Fellirex whatsoever?"

She continued to study the detective, then took another drink of her seltzer and finally replied.

"You should loosen up some, detective. Have a little fun. Sometimes, you need to go with the flow. I mean, these are bad guys we're dealing with. Sooner or later, we'll solve the case."

He rubbed his forehead and again expelled a deep breath of air.

"You've got to be kidding me. We'll … 'solve the case.' I mean, I really don't know what the hell I'm doing here now. I thought of you as something more than a common thief."

Grace swelled up a little.

"Really, detective, a common thief? Let me ask you. How much do you get paid to risk your life? Would it really hurt anyone if we supplemented that a little on the side?"

Shaking his head, he stepped back and moved toward the bridge area. Standing in the cockpit, he watched as they flew at Mach speed. Then, the cargo vessel in front of them pulled away and moved in a different direction, according to its destination. He could only see a few more transports in the distance.

He sat down in the copilot seat and eventually nodded off to sleep again.

CHAPTER FIVE:

THE KHEJARWA SALT MINES

Later, Grace walked into the cockpit and nudged the detective.

"You should wake up. We'll be landing soon."

Sitting up and rubbing his face, he glanced up at Grace.

"Landing? Landing where?"

"Khejarwa salt mines, in the Middle Eastern Commonwealth District, also known as the stairway to hell. The mines are hundreds of feet deep, and it's not the coolest place to be."

She turned and began walking toward the rear of the cargo ship.

The detective stood and followed behind. As they came to a debarking door, the humming of the engines changed, and the ship shifted while maneuvering to land.

"Uhm, lieutenant, could you try not to kill anyone else? I mean, there is such a thing as diplomacy."

She looked at him, seeming to consider his request.

"Detective, in my line of work, I generally have around ten seconds to decide if I want to use lethal force or diplomacy. I assure you, it's the lethal force that has kept me alive, not diplomacy."

"Yeah, sure, I understand. … You're accustomed to kicking the door in and blowing things and people up."

Grace smiled at this comment as if it pleased her. He continued.

"But, I'm more accustomed to using diplomatic methods. So, all I'm suggesting is that maybe you allow me the opportunity to use diplomacy first. Then, if things don't go well, uhm, I suppose you can have your turn."

As the ship landed and the engines began to shut down, Grace considered his request again. She then pinned her jacket back in a manner that gave easy access to her two lase pistols.

"Very well, detective. If you insist, I'll humor you."

She pulled her laser pistols out and flipped a switch on each one.

"Ordinarily, I don't feel it's wise to give an opponent a second chance at me, but I was considering putting my weapons in stun mode anyway."

His eyes widened. "They have a stun mode?"

She looked at him and then re-holstered the two pistols.

"Just so you know, I will defend myself. And if attacked, I'll not attempt to defend myself with diplomacy."

He nodded and raised his hands, waving them a little as if to reassure her.

"Yeah, sure, that'll be fine. Just give me a chance here. I think you'll see that diplomacy can work, and we can avoid violence."

She grimaced slightly.

Just then, a small communication port on the wall, close to the detective, lit up. A man's voice came across it.

"*Minn antel nahin cadmon. da al-aslaha ola al-aradh wastslem!*"

"The detective turned to Grace with a puzzled look. He then pushed a button on the communication device.

"Uhm, uh … this is Detective Vandenberg of the Antarctic Mining Colonies."

As he said this, Grace expelled a long breath, pulled out her two pistols and charged them.

"Detective, I suggest you step back a bit."

Grace moved behind a beam and raised her pistols into a ready position.

The detective raised his finger, signaling her to wait.

"I'm assigned to a special mission," he continued.

He then stopped, looked at Grace again and noticed her lips moving. She was whispering to herself, "six, seven, eight."

His eyes widened in fright. He stepped away from the door. It suddenly blew from its hinges. The detective was knocked back and onto the floor. Gunfire erupted, and Grace immediately stepped out from her secure spot and fired back. Several armed men fell as they tried to enter the ship.

As she stepped forward, firing repeatedly, she glanced down at the detective, who was struggling to recover from the blast. She stopped beside him.

"Come along, detective. We'll try it my way now! Maybe the diplomacy thing will work next time."

She then moved around the two men on the floor and out the shattered door as they heard more gunfire. Coughing in the haze of dust and smoke, he staggered up and stepped out behind her.

Once outside, he saw a large cavernous entrance to the salt mine.

On the disembarking ramp, Grace stood firing both weapons one after the other. Bullets and a few laser bolts hit close but seemed to have been fired from persons trying to keep low.

Stumbling down the ramp, the detective tried to get closer as Grace began to walk quickly, sensing movement to her left. She raised her weapon and fired into the overhanging rocks. Dust and chunks of the hillside fell on her attackers.

As she stepped off the ramp, a low, wheeled vehicle sped up and slid to a stop. A man with a Middle Eastern appearance jumped out of the door and aimed a weapon. Without missing a step, Grace raised a laser pistol and shot him. The man flew back several feet.

She walked up to the open door.

"Let's take this one, detective. It's all warmed up and ready to go."

Still half-ducking to avoid any additional bullets or bolts, the detective moved quickly to get into the passenger side.

"Do you know how to drive one of these wheeled things?" he asked as he climbed in.

She was looking the controls over with a puzzled expression.

"Oh, not really. But how hard can it be?"

A bullet hit the vehicle. The detective lowered himself even more.

Just as he got the door shut, Grace shoved the gear shift into reverse and with tires spinning, whipped the odd vehicle around. She then jammed the shifter into drive, and as they took off, more security vehicles came racing up to the entrance area with lights flashing.

Most continued toward the cargo vessel, but two turned around and began pursuing Grace and the detective.

As they moved farther into the expansive salt mine, the ceiling got lower and lower. Soon, they were whizzing downward in long rectangular tunnels. Holding onto the door, the detective glanced back and saw lights from the two vehicles.

"They're still behind us!"

Just as he said this, they raced into an expansive area where large machines were cutting blocks of salt from the walls.

Grace maneuvered the odd salt mine vehicle around several large but low-profile wheeled transport trucks that were moving the harvested salt toward the surface.

Sliding around in the loose powder, Grace sped around another piece of mining machinery and, coming back to the other side, raced toward her pursuers.

"What are you doing?" the detective almost shouted.

Sticking her laser pistol out the short window, Grace fired several times at the approaching vehicle. The shots took out the headlights. She pulled her arm back in just as the mining car scrapped the side and pushed them over into the path of the other vehicle. She pulled the wheel, and they slid away, sending a salty spray of powder into the air and down on the pursuing vehicle, barely avoiding a crash.

The detective groaned in fear. Holding the door with one hand, he tried to brush the salt powder off himself.

Again, she sped down another long, low tunnel. Glancing back, the detective noticed the other two vehicles were again behind them, the one with lights leading the other.

Grace floored the mining car and slid around a turn. Again, they went racing down another stretch of tunnel.

This continued for what seemed several miles, then passed through spacious areas where workers were busy mining the large blocks of salt from the walls.

Once the vehicles perusing them could no longer be seen, Grace maneuvered the vehicle through mining equipment and, finding a hiding spot in one of the mining cavities, parked the car.

"Let's go, detective." She jumped out.

Climbing out, he noticed across the cavernous mine those in pursuit now sped through at full speed and then on down the tunnels, not realizing they had just passed by Grace and the detective.

"It seems we've lost them," he said.

Grace didn't reply. She immediately took off at a quick pace across the dimly lit mine. Detective Vandenberg hurried to catch up to her.

As they came close to the tunnel leading up, Grace reached back, and taking his sleeve, pulled him into a crevasse in the tunnel wall.

Seeming perplexed, he started to say something as a large cargo vehicle crept slowly past. Before he could say anything, she pulled him toward the wheeled vehicle and jumped onto a rail on the side of the huge truck.

Struggling to get aboard, the detective jogged and then jumped up on the rail behind Grace. The two moved close to the side of the transport and held on as it traveled slowly upward, turning to a new level and then again slowly rolling along toward the surface.

After moving up several levels, they crept past a lighted room cut into the side of the tunnel. Inside, there were computers and display boards. Grace recognized this to be a control room.

Around twenty yards past the room, Grace jumped off the transport vehicle. The detective also jumped off and walked back to her. In the dim light, she moved to another pocket area of the jagged tunnel wall. She then stepped into the shadows.

"Lieutenant, can I ask you just what the hell we're doing?"

Stepping into the hollow area of the wall and beside Grace, he stared at her while she glanced out, seeming to look for any potential trouble.

"Well, I have a hunch, detective."

His eyes widened. He ran his hand through his hair and looked up in frustration.

"You have a hunch?"

She looked at him as his voice raised.

"You have a hunch? We are in the middle of a … salt mine! We're supposed to be tracking down drug dealers. But here we are, you and me, lieutenant! We stole a cargo transport, made our way to the Middle Eastern Commonwealth District, shot our way out of the stolen transport and are being pursued by the mine security guards. But it's all good because you have a hunch!"

She stared at him for several seconds before replying.

"Has anyone ever mentioned that your eyes sparkle when you're excited?"

His eyebrows raised, and he seemed to be ready to explode. He looked around the hollowed hiding spot as if to find a way out. He then turned back to Grace.

"Has anyone ever mentioned that you're totally batshit crazy, lieutenant?"

Her head moved back slightly.

"Really … detective, I believe you could have said that with a little nicer tone."

His mouth opened slightly. He shook his head in dismay.

Grace again stepped out of their hiding spot and looked around.

"I'm going to check out the control room back there. You stay here. It shouldn't take me more than ten or fifteen minutes."

He drew in a deep breath of air and expelled it slowly.

"So, why is it you're checking out this control room?"

"I told you, I have a hunch. Plus, I want to try to locate us a ride out of here."

They moved back into the hiding spot as another large cargo vehicle loaded with salt blocks crept noisily by. Once it had passed, the detective replied.

"Well, I like the idea of getting a ride out of here. I'm guessing you mean a ride away from this mine?"

She nodded a bit. "Certainly. Once I follow up on my hunch, we'll need to leave here."

He examined her with a bit of suspicion.

"Hopefully, it won't involve getting shot at again."

They looked at each other for several seconds, and he finally continued.

"Ten or fifteen minutes?"

"Yeah, it shouldn't take longer than that."

"Fine," he said and stepped closer to the wall to stay hidden.

Grace glanced down both directions of the tunnel and then moved out of the dimly lit hiding spot.

Detective Vandenberg leaned out and watched as she carefully made her way toward the control room, staying close to the jagged tunnel wall.

Once she was far enough away, the detective pulled out his comm. device and touched both ends of the small tube. The device unrolled, and he quickly called Captain Bradford.

"Hello, Captain Bradford. This is Detective Vandenberg."

"Detective! Where the hell are you?"

"We're at the Khejarwa salt mines, somewhere in the Middle Eastern Commonwealth District."

"What the hell are you doing there?"

"I don't know, sir. She says she has a hunch. Can you get me out of here? I've talked her into putting her weapons on stun mode, but we're getting shot at by security forces, and I've got a pretty good idea their weapons are not on stun!"

He leaned out to make sure Grace was not coming back. Then, he moved back as the captain replied.

"Gawd dammit! I don't need this right now. We're losing agents left and right. You've got to stay with her and try to minimize the damage. Besides that, I'll have to clear several diplomatic hurdles before I can send troops in. Can you subdue her and keep her there?"

Detective Vandenberg winced at the thought. He again leaned out and quickly back in after verifying Grace was not close by.

"No, sir. I told you, I don't believe I can do that. Regardless of any other shortcomings, the lieutenant seems quite skilled at taking care of herself. I'll do what I can. She's looking for a way out of here right now."

"Damn it all! She'll pay for this. Where is she trying to go now?"

"I don't know, sir. I've asked, but she doesn't tell me much. With all due respect, I'm just trying to stay alive … Hold on just a second, sir."

Another transport vehicle crept by. Once it was past, the detective continued.

"What about the general, her commanding officer? Maybe he can help."

"No, I've tried to contact him. He's indisposed or something, and I can't get through to him. For now, this is our problem, and the tighter the lid we can keep on it, the better. Just stay with her and try to keep me updated. I'll do what I can to get some troops there to apprehend her before she gets away again."

Detective Vandenberg expelled another breath of frustration. Before ending his conversation with Captain Bradford, he once again glanced out and down the tunnel where Grace had gone. She was nowhere to be seen.

As the detective and Captain Bradford wrapped up their conversation, Grace slipped up to the control room.

Crouching down and then easing up to the open door, she spotted two men sitting at the console. They were speaking to each other in what Grace identified as Arabic, and both wore the common, Middle Eastern head covering.

Inside the control room, one of the men stopped talking and motioned to the other to do the same. As they sat quietly, both could hear a clicking sound outside the door.

After listening for several seconds, one said something to the other and then stood and walked out the door, searching for the odd sound.

The remaining man looked at the database console and moved several numbers around with his finger.

A loud thud came from outside as if something fell to the ground, and the man turned his attention to the door.

"Hassan?" the man called out. He then stood up and cautiously moved to the door.

"Hassan?" he called out again. Then, searching outside the doorway, he stepped out.

111

Grace rose behind the man from her crouched position and, taking a step forward, stuck a small hypodermic "insta-out" shot in his neck. There was a short buzzing sound from the shot, and he fell to the ground, unconscious.

Moving into the control room, she pulled the Hacker 5000 from her jacket pocket and placed it on the console terminal. Pushing several buttons, the device began to flash red.

After this, Grace stepped back out the door and looked up and down the tunnel. Then, she moved back close to the door. Glancing back to the Hacker, she noticed the device was flashing yellow.

From the lower levels, another large cargo vehicle crept toward her and the control room. She crouched back down as it moved past her with a great deal of noise.

After the transport had passed, she looked at the Hacker and smiled slightly. It was now flashing green.

Grace then searched the two men. She took both men's comm. devices, then checked the Hacker.

For almost four minutes, the device flashed green. Then, it flashed white for several seconds and stopped flashing.

Grace moved inside the control room and picked up the Hacker. She crouched down and placed one comm. device close to the Hacker. It flashed red and then green. Once the data was pulled from that device, she hacked the other and then tossed both across the mining road.

Still kneeling and rapidly thumbed across page after page, she began to scan the information on the Hacker. After doing this for several minutes, she put the Hacker back into her jacket pocket.

Looking around the room, Grace spotted several small, unopened containers of water. Taking these and placing them in a large pocket of her jacket, she carefully moved back to the detective's hiding spot.

As she came to the nook in the wall, the detective leaned out.

"Oh, I'm glad to see you. I thought maybe you had been caught."

Grace examined him curiously in the dim light.

"What would make you think that? I've been gone almost exactly the amount of time I said I would be gone."

The detective sheepishly nodded.

"Yes, I suppose you have. Maybe we should wait here and rest for a few minutes."

Her eyes squinted, and her mouth turned down slightly.

"Detective, I'll have you know that we need to leave as soon as possible if we're to catch our departing flight."

She then turned and leaned out of the hiding spot and heard the distinct sound of a cargo vehicle moving toward them.

"Here comes our first ride."

She stepped back, and the detective did likewise. He attempted to say something, but Grace raised her hand. The slow-moving transport rolled alongside, and Grace stepped out, then jumped up on the side railing. Detective Vandenberg jogged a bit and jumped up to the railing behind Grace. They both crouched down and got as comfortable as possible.

Slowly, and with a great deal of noise and dust, the cargo

vehicle crept toward the surface, up one level, and then it turned and moved slowly around to another.

Eventually, Grace spotted daylight. She reached back and nudged Detective Vandenberg. He sat up and both watched carefully as the noisy transport slowed.

Once it reached ground level, Grace jumped off and scrambled to a hiding spot behind several large containers. The detective followed her, and both crouched for a minute as they caught their breath.

Raising up enough to get a look, Grace noticed they were on a docking area. Several huge transports were lined up and being loaded with the salt blocks. She ducked back down after scanning the situation.

"We need to get to the transport in the middle. It should be loaded and almost ready to depart."

The detective nodded in an unsure manner, but then rose enough to get a look, then said.

"I think we can move along the wall here for most of the way. It looks like we'll need to get across a short stretch in the open about twenty yards that way, but once we're past that, we can hide behind the trailers not far from the transport."

She smiled slightly.

"That's very good, detective. You're catching on quite well."

"Yeah, well, the sooner we get away from here, the better. I would rather not die in a salt mine."

The two carefully maneuvered along the rough wall. Slowly, they arrived at the trailers behind the transport, which the detective had indicated.

"We need to get aboard before they close the ramp."

Detective Vandenberg looked around at the number of busy dock personnel.

"I don't see how we can do that."

Reaching into her jacket, Grace produced four round items about the size of marbles.

"Just be ready to move when I say move."

Pressing one of the items, she then threw it to one side of the docking area. Then, she pressed another and tossed it to the opposite side. She repeated this with the other two, tossing one to each side of the busy dock.

Soon, a ruckus broke out in both directions. Detective Vandenberg leaned out and noticed smoke coming from the areas where Grace had tossed the items. Before he could move back to a hiding position, Grace moved forward.

"Let's go!" She then jogged toward the open ramp. Moving quickly behind her, the detective noticed on both sides the workers were busy investigating the sudden appearance of smoke.

The two jogged up the ramp and into the cavernous cargo area. They moved between huge stacks of salt blocks. On into the middle of the transport vessel, she led them until they were surrounded by the cargo and stood in the dim light.

Peeking around one of the rows of salt blocks, she noticed the dock workers once again preparing the vessel for departure.

"I think we made it on safely. Now, we need to find a place to hold up until we take off."

Detective Vandenberg nodded, and they moved cautiously along the rows of cargo until reaching a wall. Moving down the side, they spotted a small nook that held stowing devices and cables. The two sat on several large cable spools, and Grace pulled her Hacker out. As the detective watched for guards or dock hands approaching, she scanned the device for more information.

"I don't suppose there's a restaurant on this ship. I'm about to starve."

Grace glanced up at the detective. Reaching into her jacket, she pulled out several slim packages and handed them to him. She then reached into another pocket and pulled out one of the containers of water and handed it to him.

He studied the slim package as if it were a foreign object. Grace watched him and then said, "Field rations. They're not bad, and with the water, they'll expand in your stomach to fill you up, somewhat. At least you won't feel hungry for a while."

His eyebrows lifted a bit, and he nodded. As he began to open the package, they heard the large ramp at the back of the vessel shutting.

While Grace went back to work on the hacker, Detective Vandenberg took a bite of the rations. Soon, the engines were throttling up, and the ship vibrated under them.

Grace paid no attention to this, and five minutes later, the cargo vessel moved away from the dock and began to rise slowly into the air.

Still, Grace pecked feverishly at the Hacker, seeming immersed in the information.

After finishing the slim ration bar and taking another drink of his water, the detective observed Grace briefly before attempting some conversation.

"I suppose all we need to do now is relax and then sneak back off once we dock again."

She looked up to him, her face expressing concern.

"Well, that and keep from dying. Before long, we will be high enough that we'll either freeze to death or die from a lack of oxygen."

Detective Vandenberg sat up as Grace went back to work on the Hacker.

"What? You mean to tell me this is not a low-level cargo vessel?"

Without looking up, Grace replied.

"No, this is a sky flight, headed for a spaceport."

She glanced at the detective, who appeared to be in a slight state of shock.

"Spaceport Delta-5, to be exact."

His head shook back and forth in disbelief, then he seemed to regain his composure.

"You're telling me, we stowed away on a cargo vessel that is, at this moment, climbing higher into the sky, and within a few minutes, we will either freeze to death or die due to a lack of oxygen?"

Grace stood up and began walking along the wall of the ship. She appeared to be looking for something but still managed to reply.

"That is one possible outcome, detective. But I may have a less dire solution if I can make it work."

Following behind, the detective became a bit animated. His arms raised in the air, he almost shouted.

"If you can make it work? Lieutenant, I'm sorry to sound so pessimistic, but I've seen little that you've been able to 'make work.' I've yet to see any of the Fellirex drug we are supposed to be tracking down. You say you have a 'hunch,' but cases are seldom solved on mere hunches. And now, rather than die in a salt mine, it seems I'll die headed out to a spaceport for who knows what reason."

Grace turned to him.

"Detective, almost seventy percent of the salt from that mine is being shipped to spaceport Delta-5. Do you not find that questionable?"

She then turned and continued along the wall.

"Do I find that questionable? Lieutenant, it's a spaceport. Salt is a commodity that is sold on the inter-planetary market. Why should I find that questionable?"

Grace stopped.

"Here. This is what we need."

He looked down, and as she knelt, he could see a long hatch and a small control panel. Then, he noticed there were several more hatches past the one they were in front of.

"Escape pods?"

"Yes, they have self-contained oxygen, environment and pressure controls. If I can hack them before the vessel moves into Mach speed, we might make it."

She placed the Hacker on the control panel and, tapping several buttons, the screen began to flash red.

"I certainly hope you can do that. It's starting to get colder."

As he said this, his words came out in a vapor, indicating the temperature was dropping.

For several long seconds, the Hacker flashed red. Then, it began to flash orange. A few seconds later, it began flashing green.

Grace examined the Hacker's screen and began to input data.

"Now, if I can bypass the main system and activate these two pods, we should make it."

The detective's breath was streaming out in vapor now, and he rubbed his hands together.

"Great, yeah, that sounds super. Do you have an ETA on that project?"

She seemed to be ignoring him and continued to put data in. Then, she said, "Right about … now!"

The hatch doors on two pods opened. She looked up at him and smiled. Then, she gestured for him to climb into one.

The pods were horizontal and close to the floor. He laid down and scooted into his, then leaned over to watch Grace as she did the same.

"So, we just close the doors? It's not going to shoot me out over an ocean or something, is it, lieutenant?"

Grace looked back, and though she could not see him from inside her pod, she answered in his direction.

Well, I can't guarantee anything, detective, but I believe I have it programmed to provide life support while we are in transit to Delta-5. All you should need to do is close the hatch door. But, just in case it ejects us out over the ocean, it's been nice knowing you!"

She then shut her hatch door, and a whoosh sound emanated as if something was engaging.

With an expression of fear on his face, the detective pulled the door down. He closed his eyes, and then with a quick jerk, he shut the door. He heard another whooshing sound, and as he cautiously opened his eyes, Vandenberg could feel warm air blowing into the small escape pod.

Expelling a breath of relief, he finally relaxed. After this, it was not long before the detective was fast asleep.

Grace pulled her water container out and took a drink. Her nose twisted a little, as the pod smelled of old plastic. She then took one of the ration bars and ate it. After another drink, she pulled her Hacker out and began scanning it for information.

CHAPTER SIX:

SPACEPORT DELTA-5

After a while, Detective Vandenberg woke and pulled his comm. device out. He started to make a call but stopped and put the device back in his pocket, then laid in the reclining position for several minutes. Then, he expelled a breath of frustration and pulled his comm. device out again and tapped the number.

Seconds later, Captain Bradford answered.

"Hello, captain. This is Detective Vandenberg."

"Detective, where the hell are you? Have you been able to detain Lieutenant Wolfe?"

"Uhmm, well, I'm, or we've stowed away on a cargo sky transport headed to a spaceport. And no, I've not been able to detain the lieutenant, sir."

There was only silence. Just as the detective was about to ask if the captain was still there, he replied.

"I've sent a squad to the Khejarwa salt mines. It took some doing to get the mining officials' approval. I'm not about to tell them the rogue agent we're tracking has stowed away on one of their transports."

Before the detective could reply, the captain continued. "And the commissioner is up to his neck with problems concerning this mission. I'm not about to say anything about this now. I'll wait until we get the lieutenant arrested, and then I can give him some good news."

Again, there was silence except for the low hum of the transport's engines. Then, the captain asked.

"Do you have any idea which spaceport you're headed to?"

"Yes, sir, Spaceport Delta-5."

"Well, that's a bit of luck. I'll get a squad headed that way. They'll not get there before you and the lieutenant, but with a bit more luck, they should arrive not long after. We've had a hell of a time with this mission, detective. Every move we make, our opposition seems to have a counter move. They're very well prepared. I can't afford any more trouble from that airhead, Lieutenant Wolfe. Try to keep her as contained as possible until your backup gets there. Can you do that, detective?"

"Yes, sir, I understand. But the lieutenant is not someone who is easily contained, sir. I'll do what I can."

"That's fine, detective. I understand. Just try to prevent her from killing anyone else. I've got a crew at the East Atlanta Sky Port trying to mop that mess up. Fortunately, it seems the poor unfortunate saps she took out at the dock were into some sort of criminal activity. We're not certain just what yet. Maybe we can cover our asses on that one. But I don't need any additional messes to clean up."

"Yes, sir. I'll do what I can."

After disconnecting from the call, the detective waited for the cargo vessel to dock at the spaceport.

Eventually, the vessel's engines throttled down, and the ship seemed to be close to docking. Along with various changes in the engine vibrations, he heard loud sounds accompanied by jarring movements in the pods that gave the detective the impression they had finally reached the spaceport.

Having no experience in the situation he was in, the detective waited inside the pod. After some loud hissing sounds and more clanking noises, his pod door opened, and Grace smiled down at him.

"It's a good thing you waited until the cargo holding area had been pressurized and the floor gravitated. I completely forgot to mention that when we entered them."

He smiled sheepishly as he slid out and began to stand up.

"And what would have happened if I had not waited?"

Grace chuckled a bit, and then a sour look came across her face.

"Well, it would have been a mess, I assure you of that, detective."

She then began walking back through the long rows of salt and toward the ramp.

Detective Vandenberg hurried to catch up and was soon close behind her.

"So, why are we here again?" As he asked this, he leaned down to see through a small window. Outside, he could see they were in space, and the earth was illuminated below.

Grace ducked behind the large blocks of salt. The ramp began to open. She glanced toward the back but replied in a hushed voice.

"I'm pretty sure some shady dealings are going on here, detective. My intuition tells me there's a lot of money exchanging hands through illicit channels. Illegal stuff, you know. And I'll bet there's a lot of that illegal money stashed away here."

The detective leaned over and glanced toward the almost completely open cargo ramp. He could see several port workers lingering around the back of the ship.

"Does your intuition have any clue about how we will get past them, and how we will get away from here and back to earth?"

"Oh, I never worry much about such things. I'm sure something will develop."

His face twisted a bit. She paid no attention to him but instead watched as the workers began to walk up the open ramp.

"Come on this way," she whispered and then pulling his sleeve a little, they moved around the other side of the salt blocks.

Slowly, and being careful not to make noise, the two slipped past the workers on the opposite side of the salt cargo. As the workers moved into the ship to begin their work, Grace and the detective slipped back to the ramp and then quietly down it and into the spaceport.

Once inside, they both acted casual while passing other

workers. A few of the uniformed port workers took extra notice of Grace, but most appeared occupied with their normal duties.

Walking quickly down narrow halls, Grace seemed to have a destination in mind.

"So, uhm, do you know where we're going?"

"Well," she stopped at an intersection of two passageways, then looked down one, then the other as if getting her bearings. As a uniformed worker walked past and looked Grace over with curiosity, she replied.

"If this port is set up like the Delta-4 station, I believe the main control center is..." she looked down both directions again, then continued, "that way."

Pointing down a passage, she began walking quickly with the detective moving briskly to catch up.

"And, uhm, just why are we trying to reach the control room?"

Grace glanced back at him.

"Well, that's where all the criminals' goodies are kept. I would think you should know that."

"Goodies?" He struggled to keep up with her as she turned another corner.

"Don't worry. I'll share with you. I'm sure there will be plenty to go around."

Again, they passed by several workers who glanced at the two with interest.

"Lieutenant, I really don't want anything. In fact, I would suggest you're making a mistake."

She stopped.

"Detective, I thought we settled this. These are bad characters. It's not really like we're stealing if we're taking it from criminals … right?"

She then started walking again before he could answer.

"Well, uhm, you know I tend to differ on that assumption. If you would give me a few minutes, we could discuss this a bit."

"I'm sorry, detective, but we just don't have time for that." As she said this, she reached back and pinned her long jacket together, making her two laser pistols easily accessible. She then touched two buttons, and both began charging up.

Directly after this, they turned a corner and found two security guards standing thirty feet away and in front of a steel door.

Before the guards could do anything, Grace pulled both pistols out and shot the guards, who fell to the floor unconscious.

"Oh … damn, lieutenant!"

"Relax, detective. I've got my weapons on stun, remember? In fact, every weapon on this station should be in stun mode. We don't want to blow a hole in the wall, and all be sucked out into space now, do we?"

"No, no, we don't want that. But I just don't think this is a good idea!"

When they came to the door, Grace reached down and lifting one of the guard's hands, she held it to a screen. The door opened, and Grace dropped the man's hand and walked in. A semi-circular room with a multitude of large screens and control panels presented itself to the detective and Grace. She holstered one of her pistols.

Immediately, a guard inside noticed the two. Grace quickly shot him. As this happened, a man at the control center tapped a button, and an alarm began to sound.

"Oh, crap. This is not good!"

As the detective looked at lights flashing around the room, Grace stepped up to the control area. Several other workers stood watching as she approached the man who had hit the alarm.

"Close the door and lock it. Then, turn all the recording devices for this room off."

He stepped back a little and shook his head as if he didn't understand her.

Grace aimed her pistol at another worker and shot him. The man flew back and landed on the floor.

Now, the man she spoke to quickly turned, and after pushing several places on the console, the door closed. Then, a large screen that displayed the interior of the control room shut down.

Grace looked around the room. Spotting several cameras, she quickly shot them, causing sparks to fly and the men in the room to cover their heads as bits fell to the floor.

"Now." She pulled her small communication device out and, with her free hand, touched the ends. The device unrolled, and she again turned her attention to the man.

"I need you to open the station's financial accounts."

The man expressed surprise.

"Is this a … robbery?"

The detective lowered his head and shook it in despair.

"We'll just call it a withdrawal," Grace replied.

The man hesitated. Grace quickly pointed the pistol at the final worker in the room. As the man raised his hands in vain, she blasted him, and he flew back and onto the floor.

Once again, the man began inputting information into the console. Grace watched and then sat the communication device on a data transfer area of the console.

As this was taking place, the detective noticed something on a still-active large screen. He could clearly see armed soldiers moving down passageways. Though he didn't notice it, Grace also glanced up and saw the soldiers.

The communication device began to flash green now.

"Uhm, how much money do you want to transfer?" the man asked.

Grace reached into her jacket pocket and pulled out a small hypodermic pod. She then replied.

"Just transfer."

The man nodded.

"Yeah, yeah, sure."

Grace stepped toward the door as the man tapped the information into the console.

Stepping over to the door, Grace shot the control panel, and sparks flew from the blast and door controls. She then turned back to the screen to check where the soldiers were.

"What the hell? Is there another door out of here that I'm unaware of?" the detective asked.

After saying this, he again looked up to the screens. Grace walked around behind him and reaching up, she pushed the hypodermic pod into the back of the detective's neck and immediately injected the substance. She then hit him on the back with her free hand.

"Watch out, detective!" she almost shouted.

He wobbled a little and then stumbled as the injection took full effect. He dropped to one knee and blinked. It seemed he could barely hold himself up from falling to the floor.

After this, Grace immediately shot the remaining man as he was still entering information into the console. He fell to the floor unconscious.

Now, she took the detective by the arm and, helping him up, moved him over to a chair. He appeared drunk, as the drug put him into a barely conscious state, and he sat with a blank stare on his face.

She then reached into another pocket of her jacket and pulled out the Hacker. Holstering her pistol and stepping back up to the control console, she tapped several areas of the Hacker, put her comm. device in her pocket and sat the Hacker down on the data transfer area of the control panel. The Hacker flashed red.

She glanced up at the screens again and could see the soldiers moving down another hallway, getting closer to the control room.

The Hacker began to flash orange.

Grace moved over to the unconscious guard and took his pistol. She then moved over to the detective. Crouching, she carefully put the pistol into his hand.

"DETECTIVE!" she yelled to him.

His head bobbled, and he moaned.

Glancing back, Grace saw the Hacker begin to flash green. She turned back to the detective.

"Detective, what are you doing?" Don't make me shoot you, detective!"

He moaned again. "What…. Wha … I don … What?"

Grace sat the detective up a little. Under her breath, she whispered, "Sorry about this, detective." She then doubled her fist and hit him square in the left eye.

"Ahhgg, what the hell? What's … Wha..?" Again, he seemed to fade out and leaned forward.

Grace glanced back to the Hacker. It was still flashing green. She turned back to him.

"I told you, detective, don't try to stop me!" Grace said, almost yelling. He opened his eyes a little and moaned again.

Turning back, she saw the Hacker flash white and then stop flashing. She stood and walked over to the control panel. As she picked up the Hacker, someone banged on the door. Looking up to a screen, she saw at least ten soldiers outside the control room.

Grace touched the Hacker screen several times, and a stream of data began to scroll rapidly across it as she stood scanning the information. After watching the data race across the small screen for thirty seconds, she shut it down and locked it, then stepped back down to the detective.

The soldiers now began to work hard in their effort to break into the room. Grace heard a loud banging sound, then peered down at the detective, who wobbled but managed to stay sitting.

Looking around and up, she noticed a small nook in the corner of the ceiling rails. Grace stepped over to the corner of the room and, with one well-aimed toss, pitched the Hacker up to the nook where it landed. She looked from several angles to ensure the device was hidden well. Then, she moved back over to the detective.

Lifting the laser pistol in his hand, she pointed it toward the control console.

"Detective! Stop. What are you doing?" she said in a loud voice. The detective moaned incoherently again. Grace then reached down and fired the laser pistol in his hand several times at the control console. It started smoking, and the lights and virtual screens all went dead.

The soldiers outside were very close to breaking into the room now. Grace hurried back to the control console. She wiped her hand on an area that had been blasted with the laser pistol in the detective's hand. She then wiped her hand on her midsection. As the soldiers were just about to break down the door, she reached into her jacket and pulled one of the small, yellow hypodermic pods from the black case. She quickly put it in her mouth, drew out one of her laser pistols and then lay down on the floor and positioned herself as if she had fallen. Seconds later, the soldiers burst into the room with weapons in a ready position.

"Secure the room!" one of the soldiers said.

As several moved about the room, one went to the detective.

"Sir, are you all right?"

The detective moaned and seemed to become a little more awake.

"What? What's going on?" he asked.

"Just relax, sir," the soldier said.

Another soldier, seeming to be the leader, spoke on a comm. device, "Situation secure. Send in a medical team."

A few minutes later, as Grace lay motionless, the medical team came in and began assisting the detective and the workers. One came over to Grace and scanned her.

"Blast residue, she's been stunned."

A team came in and hoisted Grace onto a hover stretcher. As they moved her from the room, she could hear the detective talking to the lead soldier.

"I'm uh, I'm not exactly sure what happened. It's a little fuzzy. And I still feel dizzy. Did I shoot the lieutenant? Is she all right?"

"She'll be fine, sir. She was stunned like the others in the room. Everyone will be okay. It appears you got hit in the eye while trying to capture the rouge agent, sir. That'll be a shiner. No wonder you're a bit dizzy. I'll be sure to enter your actions in my report."

Grace was taken to a medical room. She was examined briefly, and then after being disarmed; she was placed on a bed in a holding cell.

Once everyone had left, Grace opened her eyes. She examined the room to be sure there was no monitoring equipment and then, taking the small pod from her mouth, she placed it in her outfit close to her left breast. She then stood up and looked out the small window on the door. She could see very little, so she lay back down and took a nap.

Grace woke to the door being unlocked. She reached into her outfit and pulling the small hypodermic pod out, quickly put it back into her mouth.

The door opened, and a military officer, along with several armed guards, stepped into the cell.

"Lieutenant Wolfe, you're being placed under arrest. I'll inform you of the charges and your rights on the way to your transport back to earth. Please stand and place your hands out in front of you."

Grace stood, and one of the guards scanned her from top to bottom. She held her hands out, and the other guard put restraints on her. She was then led out of the holding cell and to a military transport ship. Again, she was put into a small cell, and the transport departed the spaceport and headed back toward earth.

CHAPTER SEVEN:

JUSTICE SERVED

After a long flight, the military transport landed, and Grace was escorted to the mission headquarters in DC. There, she was given a change of clothes. From her sleek, skintight outfit, she changed into an orange detention jumpsuit and was locked in a secure holding cell.

Once the guards were gone, she moved to the bathroom area that was not being monitored. There, she again removed the small hypodermic pod from her mouth and placed it in her detention-issued bra.

The following morning after breakfast, Captain Bradford came to visit.

Grace stood from a reclining position on her bunk when she noticed him through the shimmering, restraining field that protected the doorway.

"Well, hello, captain! I'm a little surprised to see you. You know, I've gotten the impression you don't like me much. Isn't that silly?"

Captain Bradford frowned and exhaled.

"Always the joker, eh lieutenant? I doubt you will be laughing once you reach Fort Leavenworth."

She perked up and walked over to the door.

"Fort Leavenworth? Am I getting a transfer?"

"Lieutenant, I know you're not stupid. I know you think you're very smart, in fact. You play these little games and think you're so cute. But cute is not going to get you out of this one. So, you can do your little song and dance. But when this is over, you're going to be locked up, and they will throw away the key. And I will be very happy to see that happen."

Grace's face twisted a bit.

"Captain … I don't know if anyone has ever told you this, but you're really no fun at all."

"Is that what you were doing? Having fun? You created a path of chaos and destruction from Atlanta to Spaceport Delta-5, and I'm guessing the point of it all was to have fun?"

She studied him briefly before replying.

"Don't knock it until you've tried it," she said with a wry smile.

Shaking his head, the captain walked away.

Several hours later, a little before noon, Detective Vandenberg came to her cell.

Grace was lying down, clicking her nails together on her left hand, and didn't see him walk up.

After observing her for several seconds, he cleared his throat to get her attention.

Sitting up, Grace smiled.

"Well, hello, detective! I was hoping for visitors, but I am a bit surprised to see you here. What with all the trouble I almost got you into, I'm delighted to see you, though."

She stood and walked over to the door.

"Hello, lieutenant. I'm uh…" He looked at the force field, protecting the door and then continued. "Well, I'm glad to see you too. Though I'm a little sad about the circumstances."

Grace appeared confused.

"What do you mean, circumstances?"

He smiled a crooked smile.

"Uhm yeah, well, you know the whole … jail thing and all."

She chuckled. "Oh, yeah, the jail thing. Yeah, that is rather embarrassing. It seems taking a batch of diamonds and thousands of dollars from people that, well, 'may or may not be bad,' is not such a good idea after all!" She smiled and chuckled again.

A look of concern came across the detective's face. He looked down at his shoes and then back to Grace.

"Well, uhm, I just got back from the spaceport. I was really, kind of, well out of it for a while, and I'm still not sure what happened there at the last. I mean, I've got some blurry images floating around and a black eye."

Grace's nose scrunched up a little. Her eyes squinted in embarrassment.

"Yeah, I'm sorry about hitting you, detective. I realize now I was out of line."

"Well, that's kind of why I'm here. Could you tell me what happened?"

"Sure, and my guess would be its most likely you were disoriented when that guard glanced a stun blast off you."

He squinted.

"A what? The guard did what?"

"Yeah, I tried to warn you, and you did step out of the direct fire, but the blast caught you just a bit on the back, around the neck area. After that, you were sort of … well, you started acting a lot different."

"Different?"

"You don't remember?" she asked.

"Well, I remember you saying to look out, and then something hitting my back and, seems like my neck too."

"Oh yeah, that's how those glanced stun blasts get you … from what I understand anyway."

He stared at her, and she smiled.

"Uhm anyway, you were saying?"

Grace jerked a little, seeming to get back on the subject.

"Oh! Oh yeah, you wanted me to tell you what happened after that."

He almost frowned, but then smiled slightly, and with his eyebrows raised a bit, he nodded.

"Well, after you were hit by the guard, who I had already stunned, by the way … Remember, I mentioned not giving someone a second chance to get you?"

"Yes, I remember that, lieutenant. So, the guard woke up and shot me, but I moved, and the stun shot glanced off my back. Then, I started acting odd?"

"Well, that seems to be the case. You managed to pick up a laser pistol and stopped me. And well, I'm here and you're out there. Don't you remember any of that? You were all like, superhero and stuff."

He rubbed the side of his head. "I sort of remember. I remember you yelling at me something about not trying to stop you, but it's all real foggy."

"You know, detective, perhaps that glanced laser blast just brought out a you that you were unaware of."

His eyes squinted a little, and he studied her curiously, then nodded.

"Yeah, maybe so...I suppose. So, what's going to happen to you?"

She smiled. "Oh, I have a feeling they want to lock me up and throw away the key. I heard something about a military prison. Fort Leavenworth, I believe it's called."

The detective attempted a smile, but it turned into a look of compassion.

"I'm really sorry how things have turned out, lieutenant."

She smiled again. "Oh, don't you fret a bit, detective. You did the right thing and I ... well, I should have listened to you."

"Really?"

"Sure. You did exactly what I would expect an upstanding, law-abiding detective would do in your position. No, you don't need to worry about me. I generally make do, regardless of the circumstances. I'll most likely own that little old prison before it's all over."

He chuckled a little and smiled back at her. Then, the smile dropped from his face.

"Well, if there's anything I can do, just let me know."

She perked up.

Well, actually, there is one thing you could do for me."

He grimaced.

"If it has anything to do with breaking you out, I'll have to say no, lieutenant."

She turned her head and examined him, seeming disappointed.

"Oh … well, drat. Okay, if you can't do that, could you at least deliver a message to General Thomas's office?"

"Uhm, well, I suppose. But isn't there anyone around here, I mean in the military, who could do that for you?"

"Oh, there's only Captain Bradford. I don't know if you've noticed or not, but … well, I get the feeling Captain Bradford doesn't like me much."

The detective smiled sheepishly and nodded his head.

"Yeah, I've kind of gotten that impression too."

"And I've tried so hard, detective! In fact, the first time I met him, I offered to let him frisk me. And that's not something I let just anyone do!"

He smiled slightly again and nodded, seeming a little uncomfortable.

"Well, anyway, I'm afraid if I ask him to deliver the message, he won't do it or won't get it right."

"Oh, okay, I suppose I can do that for you. What's the message?"

"Just call General Thomas's office. It's located here in DC. Tell whoever you talk to that you have a message from Lieutenant Wolfe, for General Thomas. The message is, 'Lieutenant Wolfe requests a speedy court-martial. And she requests it by the rules of SF code 257-64.' Can you remember that?"

"Uhm, yeah, I think so."

"Repeat the code to me."

"Uh, SF 257-...."

"64!"

"Yeah, SF code 257-64."

"Repeat it again, detective."

"SF code 257-64."

"Again, the entire message."

"Really?"

"Yes!"

"Okay, uhm, Lieutenant Wolfe has a message for General Thomas. She requests a speedy court-martial according to the rules of SF 257-64."

"Good. Put it in your comm. device if you think you'll forget. I need that message delivered as soon as possible. Can you do that for me?"

He took out his comm. device and began putting the message in.

"Yeah, sure, lieutenant, I'll do it today. And, I'm sorry you're locked up. It seems I had a lot to do with that ... even though I don't remember much."

"Well, if you deliver that message after you leave here, I'll forgive you."

He nodded and seeming to have completed the note on his comm. device, he put it in his pocket and turning, nodded to her and waved.

"Goodbye, lieutenant."

"Goodbye, detective."

After he was gone, Grace lay back down on her small bunk and once again began to click her nails together.

The following morning, Captain Bradford and two security guards came to Grace's cell. As she noticed them approaching in the hallway, she stood up, turned from the monitoring cameras, pulled the small hypodermic pod from her bra and placed it in her mouth.

Once in front of the door, the captain disengaged the energy field that protected the door. Grace walked over to him.

"You must be in it deeper than I thought, lieutenant. Your court-martial is this morning. You'll need to come with us."

Grace smiled. He noticed the top two buttons of her jumpsuit were unbuttoned, slightly exposing her bra.

"You may want to tidy up before we go. It couldn't hurt your case to be more presentable."

She glanced down at her somewhat open jumpsuit.

"Oh, I like a breeze, captain. There are parts of me that just stay hot all the time. But, if you would like to button me up, I'll let you." She smiled and winked at him.

He frowned.

"Suit yourself, lieutenant. If you want to arrive at your court-martial, half-dressed, I'll let you."

He stepped aside and motioned to the guards. One stepped up and, using a small handheld device, scanned from her neck to her feet. When the scan showed a green light, the other guard produced wrist restraints. Grace held her arms out, and the guard put the restraints on her. Then, they moved out of the building and into a hovercar.

Grace was seated in a secure area at the back of the vehicle. A clear shield was in front of her to prevent any possible breakout. The guards sat in two seats in front of the protected area where Grace was seated. The seats were opposite each other, so the guards could turn back and watch the prisoner and turn their heads the other way to see the front of the vehicle. Captain Bradford sat in the passenger seat across from the driver.

When the two guards were looking away, Grace pulled the small hypodermic pod from her mouth and quickly placed it in her bra. Before her hand was completely away from her chest, one of the guards looked at her. She took the top of her jumpsuit and flapped it back and forth as if fanning her chest area, then smiled at the guard, who barely smiled back and then turned to the front of the vehicle and watched as it maneuvered through traffic.

After twenty minutes of travel through often heavy traffic, they arrived at a building with marble pillars and a lengthy entrance that led to several levels of steps.

Once out, the four moved toward the entrance. Captain Bradford led the way, and Grace, with hands cuffed in front of her, was escorted by the two guards.

Up the steps they went and into the large building, then on to an elevator and from there, down several hallways until reaching a receptionist in front of an office with a plaque on the door indicating it to be that of General Thomas.

"I'm Captain Bradford. I have Lieutenant Wolfe. We're here to see General Thomas."

The receptionist, a young woman in uniform and short, dark-brown hair, looked them over. She then touched the comm. device in her left ear.

"Sir, there is a Captain Bradford and Lieutenant Wolfe here to see you."

She looked them over again and said, "The general is expecting you. Please go in."

Stepping inside the spacious office, Grace saw the general sitting behind his large desk. As he stood up, Captain Bradford saluted him, and he returned a casual salute.

"It's good to meet you, sir. We spoke a while back about Lieutenant Wolfe," the captain said.

General Thomas looked at Grace, expelled a breath and then sat back down.

"Please have a seat. We're waiting for Commissioner Welch, and then we can proceed."

Captain Bradford turned, and finding a large sofa and several plush leather chairs, directed the guards to sit with Grace, and then he sat in one of the chairs.

After waiting a few minutes, Commissioner Welch entered from a different door that was on the side of the general's office. He was accompanied by what appeared to be a bodyguard.

"Can you please explain to me the urgency and absolute necessity of this meeting, general? I had to move several appointments around to fit this in. And I do not appreciate your calling the governor to force my attendance."

General Thomas stood, as did the captain, Grace and the guards.

"I'm sorry, commissioner. As you may be aware, we had an officer go rouge a few days ago. She requested a special court-martial according to special forces code 257-64. This is a specific option for officers in elite units, and it requires the officer's mission leaders to be present. You are, of course, the leading officer of this mission."

The commissioner looked over to Grace and frowned.

"Oh, yes, I remember her. She created a mess at our initial meeting. Well, if it doesn't take long. I have several election meetings to attended to after lunch and cannot be late."

The general nodded. "It shouldn't take long."

He then looked at Grace.

"Lieutenant Wolfe, is there anything you wish to say for yourself before we proceed?"

Grace smiled.

"Well, sir, I'm feeling a little uncomfortable with Captain Bradford and his crew here. I don't think he likes me very much. Perhaps he could state the case and be dismissed. You know, maybe he could watch the recording later."

Captain Bradford turned and glared at Grace. The general examined Grace carefully. After a few seconds, he replied.

"I'll consider it, lieutenant."

He then turned to Captain Bradford.

"Captain, please remove the restraints from Lieutenant Wolfe. For now, she's still an officer of the United States military."

"Sir, I would not advise that. I'm sure you're aware, Lieutenant Wolfe is responsible for a number of casualties and millions of dollars' worth of damage before she was apprehended."

General Thomas again seemed to be in thought. He then said, "I understand, captain, but that's an order, I'm sure Lieutenant Wolfe will act appropriately."

Grace smiled and turned to the captain with her arms held out. He grimaced and then motioned for one of the guards to remove the restraints.

Once the restraints had been removed, the general spoke out, as if talking to the walls.

"Office request, recording, please."

Several cameras lowered slightly from the ceiling. Once the small red lights on the cameras turned to green, the general proceeded.

"These are the proceedings for the court-martial of Lieutenant Wolfe from special operations."

He turned to Captain Bradford.

"Please state the charges, captain."

"Yes, sir."

The captain then pulled a comm. device from his jacket pocket and began reading a lengthy list of charges. He emphasized that Grace was responsible for casualties at the East Atlanta Sky Port. He stressed that she was also found to have several million dollars' worth of uncut diamonds on her when apprehended. He went on to state how her comm. device had almost a million dollars transferred from the spaceport financial account, then continued for several minutes with additional minor charges before finally concluding.

Grace simply stood, smiling and looking about as if somewhat uninterested in the whole event.

"All right, thank you, captain. You and your men are dismissed."

After the general said this, Captain Bradford almost choked on his words but managed to say, "Sir ... are you joking?"

"I don't joke about such things, captain. You can go now. We'll be fine."

Captain Bradford appeared to swell up a little. He grunted and turned to Grace, who smiled somewhat smugly at him.

"Sir, I object! I respectfully request you reconsider!"

"Objection noted. Now, please vacate the proceedings, captain."

Captain Bradford huffed and then motioned to the guards with his head. The three then left the room.

The commissioner watched this with a curious expression.

"Are you certain that was a good idea, general?" the commissioner asked.

"I have no reason to believe the lieutenant...." Before he could finish his sentence, Grace moved across the room in a flash and kicked the commissioner's guard square in the midsection. As he bent over in pain, she pulled the pistol from his holster and clubbed him on the head, knocking him unconscious.

General Thomas appeared shocked and stepped back.

Grace grabbed the commissioner and twisted his arm around his back, effectively putting him into a restraining hold.

"Stay put, general, or I'll blow his head off!"

She backed herself and the commissioner into a corner.

"Lieutenant, please, stay calm." General Thomas held his hands up to calm Grace.

Once in the corner, Grace reached into her bra with the hand that held the commissioner's arm. He yelled out in pain, as this twisted his arm more. She pulled the small hypodermic pod out and then popped the cap off.

With the commissioner in front of her, blocking the camera's view, she jabbed the hypodermic shot into the back of the commissioner's lower neck.

"Ahhhhggg," he yelled out. She twisted his arm higher, causing him to cry out more.

"STAY STILL!" she yelled.

"What do you want, lieutenant?" the general asked, still seeming in shock.

"I'm not going to be locked up for the rest of my life because of this dirtbag!" She turned to the commissioner. "You tell him! Tell him everything!" she almost shouted.

The commissioner grunted as if fighting something and resisting. His breathing became labored, but he began to talk. Grace lowered his arm to allow him to speak freely.

"I'm … I'm the Shadow-man. … It's me."

"What?" the general asked.

"It's me. I have a deal with the Rocasians. They supply the

Fellirex, and I supply them with salt. I use the money from the cheap Fellirex to buy rough diamonds. I use the diamonds to pay off contacts in the Khejarwa salt mines."

"But ... why? Why would you do that, commissioner?"

Grace twisted his arm again, causing him to grunt from the awkward position.

"Tell him! Tell him everything!" she said in an aggressive voice.

"All right, all right! It was to get votes. The people buying the Fellirex would be given free drugs if they voted according to the dealer's instructions. Most would be told to vote for me, but some would be told to vote for other candidates to cover the tracks. Once I was voted in as trade regent, I would maneuver to open more salt shipments indirectly to the Rocasians. They would get cheap salt, and I would gain wealth and power."

After he said this, Grace pushed him forward, and he fell onto the couch. She then took two steps and set the pistol on the general's desk. The general picked it up and pointed it at Grace.

Reaching down to the console on his desk, while keeping the pistol in a ready position, the general touched a button on the console screen.

"I need security."

Almost immediately, several armed security personnel entered the door on the side of the office. Grace raised her hands into the air.

"Commissioner Welch is under arrest. Take him into custody. I'll have the proper authorities take over. Also, take

Lieutenant Wolfe and the commissioner's guard into custody."

The security guards began to help the commissioner and his bodyguard up.

"Office request, recording off," the general said, and the lights on the cameras turned to red and then lifted back into the ceiling.

As the security guard was about to take Grace into custody, the general motioned for the man to hold up. He seemed a little confused but turned to help his fellow guard as they assisted the commissioner and his bodyguard out the door.

Once the door was closed, the general exhaled, reached into a desk drawer and pulled out a bottle of liquid that had a slight bluish glow.

"Aventian lostria. Would you like a drink?" he asked.

"Please," Grace replied and ran a hand through her hair.

The general pulled two glasses from the same desk drawer and began filling them.

"A forced confession from an officer under arrest."

He handed Grace a drink.

"Brilliant ... It'll save us six months of work ... if you have the data to back it up."

She took a drink and sat down in one of the plush chairs.

"I have it. The device is hidden on Delta-5. I also have most of the vital information memorized. But please send a reliable crew to retrieve the device. I would rather not go through another tedious data transfer session any time soon."

The general chuckled and took a drink. He then replied.

"I wasn't able to keep track of you, but I monitored Captain Bradford's activity, and wherever he sent a security team, I followed it up with a special ops squad with instructions to stay put until otherwise ordered. I'll assign the retrieval to someone on that team rather than the conventual troops."

"Good. I should also tell you that confession was prompted by Belvan truth serum. You will have around an hour and a half to interrogate the commissioner before it wears off. Also, you should act quickly. Once the commissioner's allies realize something is up, they will begin to scatter. He has associates working at the East Atlanta Port, the Khejarwa salt mines and several spaceports."

She took another drink of the lostria, then continued.

"While accessing their data banks, I also took the liberty of confiscating five million dollars from each entity. The money is loaded on the device as well. I replaced it with ghost funds, so you'll have a while before they notice it missing. If any of the companies or port officials give you problems with arresting the commissioner's associates, you can leverage the confiscated money to get their cooperation. As far as they'll know, your 'rogue agent' took the money. Returning it to them in a timely manner can depend on how cooperative they are in turning over the commissioner's agents."

The general took another drink, then rubbed the side of the glass.

"You never cease to amaze me, lieutenant. You've done

your part and then some. We'll take it from here. I wish I could give you an elaborate ceremony, along with a medal, or four or five for that matter. By now, you would have a wall full. But all I can do is give you the country's thanks and a well-deserved break. Stay close but lie low. Get some rest and return in seven days. We should have it all tied up by then, and I'll personally debrief you."

Grace nodded and then finished her drink. She held the glass and seemed to be in thought.

"Was there something else, lieutenant?"

She looked up at him.

"There was a detective who tagged along with me."

The general nodded. "Yes, a Detective Vanderbilt?"

"Vandenberg."

"Oh yes, Vandenberg."

"Well, I didn't initially plan on him coming along, but as it turned out, he was very helpful in completing the mission. Could you do something to maybe … I don't know, get him into his hometown news or something? Even though he was unaware of my mission, he did everything I would expect and hope a respectable law officer to do."

The general nodded.

"Certainly. I'll have some press releases lined up as soon as possible. By the time he gets home, he'll be a hero."

She smiled and then informed the general where the Hacker was located and the password to unlock it.

After this, Grace stood, sat her empty glass on the desk, saluted and left by the side door. She got on an elevator and then went down to her office in the basement. After getting cleaned up and changed, she went to a hotel that kept a room reserved for her. She lay down and slept for fifteen hours straight.

The seven days went by slowly and tediously for Grace. Wearing a disguise, she went shopping and attended several live shows but was relieved when the week finally ended.

Dressed in a tight-fitting, white and peach-colored outfit, she arrived at the large building with marble pillars.

In General Thomas's office, she heard how the Hacker had been retrieved, and the mass of evidence against the commissioner and his associates was used to make hundreds of arrests. It was also explained that the commissioner had been thrown a curveball when the initial meeting room had been changed to accommodate Grace's requested lunch. As the general explained it, the Roca stealth device had to be moved through the venting system to gain the facial recognition imprints.

As she sipped her drink, the general concluded that the commissioner had the advantage with the information the stealth device relayed before Grace destroyed it. As the agents were sent out to follow up the leads, their faces revealed their approach, and evidence was either destroyed or successfully relocated. The agents became sacrificial lambs, and without Grace wrapping the case up quickly, many more would have been killed or wounded.

After the debriefing, Grace took the elevator to the ground floor. As she was moving toward the exit, she pulled her handbag up and searched for her sunglasses. As she did this, she passed someone who quickly turned around and walked back to her.

"Lieutenant?"

Grace stopped and, looking up from her handbag, saw Detective Vandenberg in front of her with a look of shock.

"Oh … umh … hello, detective. What on earth are you doing here?"

He seemed to be at a loss for words. He looked her over in an effort, it appeared, to believe his eyes, and then clearing his throat, he replied.

"I, well, I was coming to try to talk with the general. I went to the cell they had you held in, and they said you were gone and didn't know where you might be. I talked to Captain Bradford, and he said you were likely locked up at Fort Leavenworth. So, I thought I might try to talk with the general, hoping he could tell me where you were."

Grace smiled somewhat apprehensively.

"Well, I'm flattered, detective. But why would you want to see me after all the trouble I almost got you into?"

"Well, I just … Oh, I don't know, lieutenant. It seems I'm turning into some sort of hero back home. My parents saw something on the news about me helping take down a rogue agent."

He looked her over again from top to bottom.

"So, it seems you didn't get locked up? How did you manage that?"

Grace now appeared uncomfortable. She glanced around and then took a deep breath.

"Well … detective, you should never underestimate the power of a string bikini."

He laughed a little, and she chuckled as well.

Becoming serious again, he looked to the floor and then back up to her with a sad expression.

"Well, it seems you're no longer in the army. I suppose that's better than being locked up."

She looked down at her civilian outfit.

"Oh, yeah, well, it's certainly better to be out of a job than to be locked up."

They both laughed nervously again.

"So, how's the mission going? Shouldn't you be working now?"

"Oh, that. Well, it … the mission, it's done, I mean, completed. And I'll be heading back to the mining colonies tomorrow."

"Really?"

"Yeah, well, it seems one of the teams made some sort of breakthrough four or five days ago. Yeah, it was odd. After I visited you in your cell, I went back to work at headquarters. From everything I heard, we were losing agents left and right. It was going very badly. Then, out of the blue, the word came that there had been a breakthrough with one of our teams, and everything just started wrapping up from there."

"Oh, well, that's nice … And to think, I almost got us killed because of a silly hunch."

Detective Vandenberg smiled, and Grace smiled, but still seemed uncomfortable.

Running his hand along the side of his head, he started to speak at the same instant Grace did.

"Well…"

"So…"

"I'm sorry. Go ahead," he said.

"I just wondered about you trying to visit me again."

He again looked down at his feet and then replied.

"Well, it's just that … Well, even though we almost got killed … several times. It was, well, it was the most exciting thing I've ever done. I didn't realize it until I was certain I wasn't going to die. But after things calmed down, I realized how exhilarating it was."

Grace smiled now and appeared to calm some.

"Yes, well, you'll certainly have some stories for the grandkids."

He laughed, and she did too.

"Yeah, I think I'll be able to go home and live contently with my dull job now."

Again, they both laughed a bit. He then continued.

"Another reason I wanted to see you again was … well, you know what I said back at the salt mines about you being crazy?"

She nodded.

"Well, I apologize for that. I've thought about everything, and I think there's still something about you that, well, that no one else sees."

Grace tensed up a bit. The detective continued.

"I don't know what it is, and it doesn't really matter, but I'm sorry I said you were crazy. I don't think you're crazy.

Maybe extremely eccentric? But I'm sorry I said that, and I wanted to see you before I left and to apologize for that."

Grace exhaled and relaxed again.

"Apology accepted, detective. And, just for the books, I've become accustomed to being called crazy. Actually ..."

She leaned over to him to whisper something. He moved closer. She spoke softly.

"I prefer it when people think I'm crazy. I've found it to be the best method of keeping them out of my way."

His face twisted with a puzzled expression. Grace straightened back up and smiled brightly.

"Goodbye, detective. It was nice working with you."

She then walked away as he stood watching. He rubbed the side of his head and then again looked up toward her, seeming to have had a slight revelation.

Grace continued out the front and into the bright sunshine. She put her sunglasses on and then hailed a hover cab. From there, she made her way back home to Las Vegas.

CHAPTER EIGHT:

FLEETING HAPPINESS

It was afternoon before Grace wearily made her way to the elevator of her apartment building. She stepped in and touched the button to the top floor.

Stepping out of the elevator, she went down the hall and opened the door to her half-finished apartment. She loved the incomplete feel of her home. It seemed to fit her life. When she rented it, the work was supposed to be done in a few months, but it stopped for some reason, and after a while, she told the owner she would pay the same rent if it was left unfinished. He agreed.

Tossing her bag on the couch, she then stepped out the door and into the open and unfinished area. The breeze was constant this high up. She stepped over to the large metal ring and hopped out to it. It swung around, and she held on. Then, she slipped in the center and positioned herself in a reclining manner. The streets of Las Vegas bustled far below.

For twenty minutes or so, she sat watching the activity around her. She took in another deep breath and then pulled herself up and hopped back to her apartment.

Soon, she had cleaned up and thrown on a long sleeping shirt. She turned on some light music, made herself a drink and sat on the couch.

Ten minutes later, she got up and made another drink. Before she had sat back down, the door chimes rang.

With drink in hand, she moved to the door. Pressing a button, it became transparent. Doctor Reese stood in front of her apartment. She pushed the button again, and the door went dark. She then opened it.

"Hello, Brad. Or should I call you 'Doctor Reese?' I'm not in the mood to call you 'Father,' so give that notion up right now."

Doctor Reese stepped inside.

"Grace, I'm glad to see you too. I've been concerned about you, but I always am while you're on a mission."

She stood watching him for several seconds, then took a drink.

"Come on in. I was actually feeling a bit lonely."

She walked toward the living room. Then, she sat down on the couch and held her drink close to her chest.

Doctor Reese came in and sat in a chair across from her.

"Would you like a drink?"

"Maybe later. … So, how did the mission go?"

"Same as usual."

He thought about this before replying.

"Let me guess. You saved the world, and only you and General Thomas know anything about it?"

She studied him again.

"You always seem to know when I'm back from a mission. Other than calling on me to be sure I'm 'okay,' what brings you?"

Doctor Reese readjusted himself in his chair.

"Well … I just wanted to see you. I've missed you."

Grace appeared to swell up. Her lips tightened. She downed the remainder of her drink, stood up and walked over to the dispenser. As she began to make another drink, she replied.

"I didn't plan on getting drunk tonight, Brad. But suddenly I have the urge to just get shitfaced drunk. How about we both just get so drunk we can't stand up? Would you do that with me?"

He turned to look at her.

"Grace, I wish you wouldn't drink so much."

Now, she appeared to come unglued. She walked over to him and pointed her finger in his face.

"STOP IT! DAMN YOU! STOP IT RIGHT NOW!"

She walked away from him, stood looking at the wall and took another drink.

"You know why I drink. You know why I hang around the ghetto districts when I'm not working. … You know why I do everything I do. So, just stop the acting, damn you."

She turned around and looked at him.

"I'm not your daughter, Brad. Stop pretending to be my father. She was not my mother. You cloned me from your dead wife. You made me in your lab. Yeah, you say I'm better than she was. I have a Kev-tech, military-grade skeletal structure that is a hundred times stronger than normal bone. I have a hybrid Croill-Z700 processor in my head that interacts with my organic brain. I can process information faster than you can blink an eye. But the rest of me is woman, Brad. The rest of me feels and thinks the same as she did. I see what she saw in you. And don't give me that shit about, 'You're old enough to be my father.' I woke up in the lab a twenty-year-old woman. I don't have a past, all I had to start with is what was programmed into my…" she tapped the side of her head, "my cyborg brain!"

He winced a bit.

"Grace, I wish you wouldn't use that phrase."

She looked at him with an expression of shock.

"You wish I wouldn't use that phrase? Really, that's supposed to help? So, if I don't call myself a clone, or a cyborg, I'll feel better? Will that make me feel more human, Brad? Is that your answer to my emptiness?"

He sat silently as she ran her fingers through her hair. She began to cry and turned back to the wall.

"I think I'll have that drink now," he said.

"Help yourself," she mumbled.

Standing up, Doctor Reese went to the drink dispenser. He selected a martini from the glowing selection display. Several seconds later, with his drink in hand, he moved closer to her. Though still a few feet away, he could tell she was still crying. He took a drink.

"Grace, I'm sorry."

She turned to him. Her eyes were slightly swollen and damp from tears.

"You're sorry?"

"Yes, I'm sorry for hurting you. I'm sorry for asking you to … pretend. It's difficult for me too."

"It's difficult for you? You have no idea. Do you suppose waking up a fully grown and developed woman in your laboratory was easy? I had all the information needed to keep me from going into shock, but it was not easy."

She walked over to the drink dispenser and topped off her glass. Taking another drink, she turned to him.

"Brad, I don't care about the age difference. I see everything in you that she saw. Damn it! I was cloned from her! Why do you insist we play these … stupid games? Why do you?"

She began to cry again. He walked over to her. He took her drink and sat it and his drink on the counter. She looked into his eyes. He took her into his arms. They kissed. She laughed a little and then kissed him again, passionately.

They moved to the bedroom and lay on the bed. Soon, they were making love. They shared each other through the evening and night. Neither slept until a few hours before sunrise.

Around ten in the morning, Grace woke, and she was the only one in bed. She sat up quickly and looked around.

"BRAD!"

"Yes, I'm coming."

She expelled a sigh of relief.

He came into the bedroom holding a tray with a home-cooked breakfast.

Grace laughed aloud and put her hand to her mouth.

"Oh, you are a sweetheart!"

Brad sat down beside her on the bed. She held her finger up and then got out of bed completely naked. She went to the bathroom and soon came out with a short robe on.

Looking the tray over, Grace picked up a piece of toast and began eating.

"I'll get us some coffee," he said and was soon heading for the small kitchen.

Later, Grace reclined in bed with her coffee, and Brad sat on a chair not far away. She looked to him and smiled brightly as she smelled her coffee, then took a sip.

"Are you happy?" he asked as her cup lowered.

"Very," she answered.

"Good." He also took a drink, then lowered the cup to his lap.

"Happiness can be a fleeting thing, Grace. I've had some experience with that—again, and again it seems. I have happiness for a brief time, and then it's gone."

She studied his face and then moved to the side of the bed and still sitting, asked, "Why did you wait so long for this? Why did you prevent our happiness, Brad? I love you, just as she loved you. The only thing that has been real in my short life has been you. Every time I see you, it's as if I connect with her. I feel that I have a past, and now I feel that I have a future."

His face twisted slightly as if in pain. He sat his coffee on a small side table, then stood, walked a few feet from the chair and then turned to her.

"The questions … they always come too soon."

"What? What are you talking about?" she asked.

He ran his fingers through his hair. Took a deep breath and exhaled. Then replied.

"You are just the same as she was, Grace. I've always had trouble understanding how we fell in love so fast and so completely. She was thirty-one, and I was thirty-two. I don't think either of us saw it coming. We met at Fort Campbell, where I was working on a project for the army. It was love at first sight for both of us."

Grace rested her coffee cup on her leg and leaned back, holding herself up with one hand. Brad continued.

"She was a decorated special operations captain. I was just a professor and scientist. I was never an extremely brave person. I had trouble understanding how such a brave warrior could love me so dearly. But we both felt so much love for each other that nothing else mattered."

"We were married, and for a brief time, it was just about our love for each other. But then, as she went on mission after mission, I began to realize how dangerous her line of work was."

He looked at Grace. She expressed interest and concern. He continued.

"As time went by, she became injured on several occasions. I was so afraid for her. I begged her to transfer to an administrative job. But she was, as you are. She was born a much higher caliber than the average person. She lived on the edge and could not survive at a desk or in an office. She had to be where the action was. I know that now. And I know it's why you spend your off time in the ghetto districts. You must be on edge. It's where you're most comfortable. Sure, after a mission, you can relax for a short period. But you will return to the edge no matter what. It's a part of you, and it was a part of her."

He came back to the chair and sat down. She sat her coffee on a table beside the bed. He looked at her and continued.

"Grace, it was our love that led to her death. I know it distracted her from the razor's edge that she lived on. It was the outside element that eventually shifted the balance and cost her life."

She stared at him for several long seconds, then stood up and turned away from him. She ran her fingers through her long hair, then turned back to him.

"You don't know that, Brad. You can't be certain that she was distracted by love. How can you know that?"

He picked up his coffee and took a drink as she watched. He took a deep breath, sat the cup back down and looked up at her.

"I'm a scientist. I deal with numbers and averages. I calculate odds and percentages. I've gone over it again and again. It was after we were married that she started slipping. The numbers all indicated that our love and marriage were what offset the balance in her work. I would not accept that if I didn't feel certain it was so. Believe me, I wanted any answer other than that one. I've run the numbers repeatedly, hoping and praying for a different outcome."

Her face became tense from the thought. She shook her head, seeming not to want to accept it. She turned away from him. Then after a few seconds, she turned back with tears welling up in her eyes.

"I'll … do something else. I'll leave the service and find a peaceful job. I can do that."

Brad stood up and expelled a long breath. He walked over and gently wiped a tear from her cheek.

"I wish it were that simple. I really do. But a tiger can't change its stripes. You're something special. She was something special. The world needs heroes and people to save their … sorry asses. She did that, and now you do it."

He turned away from her and then continued.

"When the government offered me to clone her, when they offered me to make you, I jumped at the chance. They knew they would need my approval to do such a thing, and by me being able to do the work, it was a perfect fit. But, as you lay in the incubation pod, developing at an accelerated rate, I began to realize the truth. And that was, I could not survive losing her again. It almost killed me losing her. It would kill me to lose you."

He walked over and sat on the edge of the bed. She came over and sat down, facing him.

"What are you saying?"

"I'm saying. The world needs you the way you are—a wonderful, dangerous warrior who fights for good. I need you too. And you need me. But we can't have it all. I can't let you do your job and become distracted as she did. We can only have a little happiness, in-between, because you belong to the world, the way you are."

She moved closer to him.

"Brad, don't you understand? I won't let you go. I'm better than she was. You said it yourself."

"Yes, you are better than she was, physically and mentally. But love is an emotion. We can't cover that potential risk. She could not remove me completely from her mind while she was out there saving the world, and you wouldn't be able to either. I know that. I've crunched the numbers, and they always come out the same."

Again, she shook her head as if to change his words.

"Brad, I love you. I won't let you go now that I finally have you! I won't!"

He smiled. Then, he leaned over and kissed her. She smiled.

"I know you won't let me go voluntarily. That's why I installed a failsafe."

Her head twisted slightly in confusion. He continued.

"It's a combination of hypnosis and programming in your synthetic, synopsis processor."

Her eyes squinted slightly.

"Brad?" she asked in a soft voice.

"I'm so sorry, Grace..."

"His voice changed as if talking to someone else.

"Enact protocol Venus, 47986J."

After he said this, Grace fell back onto the bed, completely unconscious.

After staring at her for a brief minute, he gently moved her to a sleeping position. Then, he sat and gently stroked the long dark hair from her face. A tear fell and landed on the sheets. He leaned over and kissed her head.

Doctor Reese then took their coffee cups and breakfast dishes into the small kitchen. He went back to the front door and opened it. Outside and beside the doorway, there was a sack that he had put there before ringing the doorbell the night before. He picked it up and brought it in.

Once inside, he pulled two half-full bottles out. They had slightly glowing pink liquid inside, and he sat one on the table beside her bed. Then, he opened the other and putting a little liquid on his hand, he reached down and daubed his hand to Grace's robe and a little on her cheek.

The doctor then put the top on the second bottle and set it on the counter by the drink dispenser.

After this, he went to the kitchen and cleaned all the dishes. He got dressed and made certain there was no evidence of his having been there. Finally, after a last look around, Brad Reese quietly left the apartment, locking the door behind him.

Several hours later, Grace was awakened by the chiming of her comm. device. She stirred in the bed as it chimed over and over, indicating an incoming call.

Groaning aloud and finally reaching over to the table, she pushed a link button, and a holographic picture lit up. It was Doctor Reese.

"Grace, hello. Are you there?"

She moaned again and then rolled over to where she could see the image of Doctor Reese looking at her.

"Grace, are you still in bed? It's way past noon."

"Yes, well, I was sleeping very well until a minute ago."

She sat up and rubbed her head.

"Are you okay? I heard you were back from the mission, and I wanted to check on you."

She looked around the room, seeming to be in a daze.

"Uhmm, I'm … Well, I seem to have forgotten."

"Forgotten what? Are you all right?"

She still expressed confusion.

"Uhmmm, how did I get home? The last thing I remember is leaving DC."

"You don't remember last night? Grace, have you been drinking Kelluargan wine again?"

She looked at the table and picked up the half-empty bottle.

"Grace! You know what that does to you! I know you're very fond of it, but you know how it causes you to lose your memory. … Grace, there's no one else in your bed is there?"

She turned and looked at her bed. "No."

"Thank goodness."

She lowered her head and sniffed her robe, then sat the bottle of glowing pink liquid back on the table.

"How is it you always seem to know when I finish a mission, Brad?"

"Brad, again? Grace, we discussed this."

She ran her fingers through her hair again.

"Yeah, yeah, whatever, FATHER! I've got a headache, and I'm not in the mood to debate with you."

She stood up.

"I need a shower, daddy dearest!"

"Grace, you're okay, though, other than having a hangover?"

She started toward the bathroom.

"Yeah, I'm fine, Doctor Reese! Not a scratch on me. Thanks for your concern!"

He watched her as she pulled the robe off and dropped it to the floor before entering the bathroom. His face expressed sadness as he heard the water turn on. Finally, he touched the button to end the call.

Six weeks later: Phoenix Arizona, Ghetto District.

"So, all I have to do is hit that little thingy in the middle, with five of these ... what did you call them?"

"Darts, sweetheart, they're called darts."

Grace smiled and examined the small dart with interest. She was dressed in skintight, white leather leggings and a tight corset-styled, pink top that flattered her cleavage.

Around her in the large, dimly lit tavern were at least twenty people, mostly men, but a few women. All watched as a man seeming to be the leader stood beside Grace and continued to eye her from top to bottom.

"And you said if I hit the circle in the middle, I get to throw another dart?"

As she said this, she noticed a man about twelve feet away, licking his lips to her over and over.

"Yeah, darling, whatever you want. You keep shooting as long as you hit the bullseye. But when you miss, it's my turn."

She smiled but watched the man across the room from the corner of her eye. He continued licking his lips and began to make a slight humping gesture toward her.

"Well, I don't know."

She began making a throwing motion with the dart as if testing her ability to use it.

"You know, I really need the money and all, but you're most likely better at this game than I am. And if I lose … It's, well, I'm just one girl, and there's a lot of you."

She continued to make a throwing motion as the leader smiled with glee and started to reply. Before he could, though, Grace made a quick throwing motion, and the dart left her hand. It went flying across the room and hit the man that was licking his lips square in the crotch.

"Aaaggghhhhhhhh!" The man grunted in pain and bent over. Everyone other than the man and Grace erupted in laughter.

"Ohhh! Ohhhh, oppssieee! I'm sorry!"

She moved over to the man.

"Here, let me help you!"

Almost in shock, the man raised his hand for her to stop, but she reached down and grabbed the dart, then stumbled in her high-heeled boots and seeming to almost fall, jammed the dart in farther rather than pull it out.

"Aagggggg. Get away from me, you … stupid broad! What the hell?"

The man looked down at the now deeply embedded dart

as she backed away. What could be called a high-pitched squeal erupted from his mouth and lasted for several seconds.

He painfully straightened up but still stared at the dart in his groin area. He moaned again in agony and taking the dart, pulled it out with one quick move. He again squealed and dropping the dart on the floor, he turned and waddled toward the restroom.

"Will he be okay?"

The leader stepped up to her, still chuckling, and handed her another dart.

"Sure, he'll be fine. Maybe not in time for tonight's activities, but that'll be good for the rest of us. Like you said, you're only one girl. Now, can we get this little game over with? You know, good old Mr. Lewinski will be waking up soon, and you'll want to get that money back into his account before he finds out you've been embezzling."

Grace walked back over to her position in front of the dartboard. Just then, a jingling sound came from her chest area.

She looked down, and the leader also looked at her chest. The jingling sounded again.

"Uhm, could you excuse me just one minute?"

Grace pulled on a gold chain around her neck, and from her corset top, a small cylinder came out at the end of it. She smiled and touched both ends causing it to unroll into her comm. device.

Lifting her finger, she motioned for them to wait, and then, with the entire group watching, she stepped a few feet away.

"Hello?"

"Lieutenant Wolfe?"

"Noooo … this is Happy Horny Toad Hotel. Can I help you?"

"Lieutenant Wolfe, this is Major Eneken."

Grace winced. She looked back at the group watching and once again raised her finger to indicate they should wait just a minute.

"Major Eneken. Why do you always call at the worst possible times? I have a group of people behind me expecting a wild, eight-hour orgy with me being the star, and then you call. How do you manage to pick the worst times to call?"

"Lieutenant Wolfe, as you're aware, I would rather never call you. In fact, if I could never, ever disturb your extravagant and overindulgent lifestyle, it would be perfectly fine with me. But for some unknown reason, General Thomas has insisted I call you in from disciplinary leave and assign you to this mission."

She looked back at the group of people and then asked.

"What is it about, major?"

"I'm to direct you to a location where you will be briefed on the mission."

"I'm not going anywhere until you tell me what it's about!"

There were several seconds of silence, then an exasperated groan. Finally, the major replied.

"Fine, well, all I can tell you right now is there's a crisis with our lunar colonies."

She perked up.

"A crisis with our lunar colonies?"

"Yes, but that is all I can say, lieutenant. You will need to report to the briefing location for the full mission report."

She stood in thought for several seconds.

"Okay, but could you just call me back in five minutes, major?"

Again, she heard a disgruntled moan, then he replied.

"Five minutes, lieutenant. I'm starting the clock now."

She rolled the device up and stuck it back into her cleavage as she walked over to the position in front of the dartboard.

"I'm sorry to have to cut this so short, but it seems I'm needed on the moon."

She quickly threw one dart after another until five darts were lodged in the bullseye of the board.

Everyone stood in shock, examining the dartboard in disbelief. Then, a chiming sound caused the leader and the others to turn and see Grace by his comm. device. She was holding her device up, and it had a green light flashing. On the screen was a transfer amount of thirty-six thousand dollars.

Grace smiled somewhat coyly and said, "Thank you for your patronage!"

The End

Thank you for reading Sane Grace. We hope you enjoyed it.

You may be interested in other books by Oliver, including the Metaphysical & visionary / Urban fiction, Spyder Bones. For your convenience we've added a preview.

For a complete listing please check out all of Oliver Phipps' works online.

SPYDER BONES

Gray Door Ltd.

CONTENTS

End of preview***************

CHAPTER ONE:

Look! A Soldier of Light

Aaron stepped out from the army PX. He pulled the small specialist class four insignia pins from the paper bag. There were eight sets on the card. Pulling two from it, he reached up and removed the corporal insignia from his collar and replaced them with the specialist insignia.

Placing the corporal pins on the card where the specialist pins had been, Aaron put it back in the sack and began walking down the sidewalk toward his barracks.

Fort Hood was busy, and he waited as several large trucks moved past before he chanced crossing the street.

The summer of 1969 was beginning as a hot one. The slight breeze barely gave Aaron any relief.

After a short walk, the young soldier stepped inside his barracks. The building was much cooler, and he quickly pulled his hat off. He then passed by the CQ desk and jogged up the stairs to his quarters.

Opening the door, he found a young private standing in the middle of the room, seeming a bit lost. He had his gear and duffle bags all around him and looked surprised when Aaron entered the room.

"Hello, corporal," the private said and then, noticing the specialist insignia, said, "Oh, uhm, I thought this was Corporal Prescott's room."

"I'm Corporal Prescott or was Corporal Prescott." Aaron then extended his hand to the young private.

"Oh, well, it's nice to meet you. I'm Wilson, or Mark Wilson. I mean Private Wilson."

Aaron smiled and briefly recalled his first few months after boot camp.

"Well, it's nice to meet you, Private Wilson. I suppose we're roommates for the time being?"

"Yes, sir, I mean corp... specialist."

"Well, that's good. And the reason my rank changed is that I changed my MOS from cavalryman to combat medic. I recently finished my training, but most of the guys around here have only known me as a corporal."

Private Wilson nodded, but still appeared lost.

"So, you've been over there, right?" the private asked.

Aaron moved over to his locker and opened it. He glanced back at the private and then sat his paper sack on a shelf.

"Vietnam?"

The private nodded.

"Yeah, two years as a cavalryman, and now I've re-upped as a medic."

The young man appeared shocked.

"You re-upped? Really? Why?"

Aaron moved around the private, sat on his bunk, and looked up at Mark.

"I re-enlisted for two more years because I like the army. Is that so surprising?"

"You mean… you weren't drafted to begin with?"

"No, I volunteered."

The private appeared even more astounded. His eyes were wide, and he stared at Aaron.

"If I wasn't drafted, I wouldn't go. I mean, I heard it's really bad."

Aaron smiled. "Oh, it's not bad all the time."

The young private gave him an odd look but quickly recovered.

"So, is that my locker then?" he asked, pointing to the one beside Aaron's.

Aaron nodded and began to help him get settled.

The following day, Aaron and Mark were sitting in the recreation room watching television. Not far from them, several young soldiers played a game of pool.

A husky soldier walked into the room. Upon seeing Aaron, he shouted out.

"Hey, Spider!"

Aaron looked back, and as a smile broke across his face, he jumped up and moved toward the burly soldier.

"Anderson! You…old skunk, what are you doing here?" Aaron then shook the soldier's hand and grasped his arm.

"Oh, I thought I might give the Vietcong another chance to do me in. I don't think they can. But you know me, I'm a betting man!"

Aaron looked at him closely. His face tightened a bit.

"So, it has nothing to do with Hue?"

Anderson's eyebrows raised.

"What? Naa, no more than you re-upping has anything to do with Ping."

Aaron smiled. "Actually, Ping has a lot to do with me re-upping, but I'll be sure to tell Hue that she had little to do with you re-enlisting."

Anderson's face turned grim. "You better not, Spider, if you know what's good for you."

Both laughed. Then, Aaron introduced him to Private Wilson. The young private smiled meekly.

"Well, Private Wilson. You should know that Spider here is one hell-uva corporal. I've been through it with this one, and he's the best."

After Anderson said this, Private Wilson replied, "Specialist, you mean?"

Anderson glanced at Aaron's collar.

"What the hell? What's going on?"

Aaron appeared a bit embarrassed. Anderson continued.

"Wait, you did it, didn't you? You went and did it. You changed your MOS, didn't you?"

"Yeah, I told you I was going to," Aaron replied.

"Man, why would you ruin a perfectly good soldier career by becoming a medic? Now, I'll have to call you 'Doc,' or 'Bones,' or something like that. Honestly, I liked you as Spider."

Aaron smiled again.

"I wanted to do something else. Actually, I've been

wanting to do it for a while now." He then patted Anderson on the arm. "I'll see you later. I'm sure glad one from our troop came back. I was beginning to think I would be the only one."

Anderson nodded. "Yeah. Well, there's not many wanting to go where we're headed, and even fewer that are crazy enough to go back once they've been there."

With that, Aaron left the recreation room.

Once he had gone, Private Wilson asked, "Why do you call him Spider?"

Anderson chuckled. "That man was the most successful tunnel rat in our unit, private. He would take two Colt 45s into a Vietcong tunnel and clear it out. Then, we would laugh and say he looked like a "spider" when he came crawling back out. So, we started calling him Spider. Make no mistake, private. That's one of the bravest or craziest men you'll ever meet. You did well to end up in a unit with him."

Private Wilson nodded with an impressed expression.

Over the next week, the squad replacement group filled out. Most were new soldiers that had been drafted, though a few volunteered.

There were also a few that had re-enlisted as he and Anderson had done, but in this group, only the two veterans remained. From Aaron's squad, some had been killed, several were wounded and not able to fight any longer, and around half had made it to the end of their enlistment in one piece.

Two weeks later, the cavalry soldiers boarded the first of several long flights and layovers. A few days later, Aaron and his fellow soldiers stepped off the back ramp of a large transport plane and set foot on the southeast Asian soil of Vietnam.

Anderson took in a deep breath and exhaled.

"Mmmm, sweet tropical flowers with just a hint of napalm. Smells like home."

Aaron chuckled as he struggled with the bulky gear and walked past his friend.

"What are you laughing about, Bones? You're glad to be back too. You don't fool me." Anderson said.

Aaron stopped and looked back. "Would you stop calling me Bones?"

"Nope, I've decided you don't look like a 'Doc,' so Bones will have to do."

"I kinda liked Spider," Aaron replied and then began walking again.

Anderson hoisted his duffle bag onto his back and, grabbing his other gear, fell in behind Aaron.

"Yeah, well, I told you not to do that medic thing. You see, that's what happens. You changed your job, and now you get to be Bones instead of Spider. It's not like I didn't warn you."

Aaron glanced back at his friend. He gave him an odd expression but continued his departure from the runway.

The rest of the day was spent getting settled in. The officers were glad to see a few seasoned soldiers among the otherwise green troops.

That afternoon, Aaron and Anderson requested a pass for Saturday, and to their surprise, each received one.

Several days later, the two rode in a taxi to Saigon. Anderson teased his friend along the way.

"I'll bet Ping has forgotten all about you. She's probably already got her another GI. I'm guessing a jarhead or a sailor."

Aaron studied Anderson as the car darted through traffic. The taxi driver laid on the horn and shouted something in Vietnamese to another driver.

"So, you don't think Hue has her another steady?" Aaron asked, once the vehicle seemed to be out of harm's way.

"Oh, I'm sure she does. You see, I've already come to that conclusion. A sweet gal like Hue attracts 'em like honey. But, once she knows I'm back, she'll drop them deadbeats like rotten tomatoes."

"Well, maybe I've come to the same conclusion about Ping," Aaron replied.

"Yeah, right! You can't fool me, Bones. You're ga-ga over Ping!"

"Bones again? Why can't you just call me Spider?"

The taxi swerved again, and both men held the door.

"Nope, you're Bones now. I already told you not to do the medic thing. But no, you had to go and ruin a perfectly good cavalryman to be a medic. So, you're Bones now. Learn to like it."

Aaron grimaced slightly as the small car pulled up to a nightclub. Anderson's attention turned to the music and laughter emanating from within the building as Aaron paid the driver.

When the two soldiers walked into the club, they were met with a thick haze of cigarette smoke and blaring dance music.

Pushing through a mass of American GIs, they came to a large open room. A stage area ran along the walls, and on the stage were beautiful Vietnamese women. They all wore skimpy outfits or bikinis and danced to the music being played.

The men shouted or whistled at the women, and very often, one of the dancers would need to step back as a soldier or marine would try to touch a woman's leg.

Aaron looked through the smoky haze, searching for Ping. Finally, he spotted her on the stage area to his far left. He nudged Anderson.

"Oh yeah! There's Ping. Do ya see Hue?"

"No, but I'll ask Ping about her...if I can get her down from the stage."

As the two came closer to the attractive and petite Vietnamese woman on stage, Ping let out a scream. She began to wave and, moving carefully in her high heels, maneuvered past the other women and then down some steps.

"SPIDER!" She yelled and then pushed a soldier away who was trying to get his hands on her.

Ping weaved through the crowded club and landed in Aaron's arms. She immediately gave him a kiss on the lips and then, pulling away from him, slapped his face.

"Hey," Aaron rubbed his cheek as several soldiers around them, including Anderson, laughed.

"You make me worry, Spider. Where you been? You know I can't wait forever."

"I told you it would be three months, Ping."

As Aaron said this, a Vietnamese man came over and started chattering and pointing up to the stage.

Ping chattered in Vietnamese back to the man, who appeared to be the manager.

"I got to go back work."

"Hey, where's Hue?" Anderson asked as she turned and began to make her way back to the stage.

"She backstage. I tell her you here. She be so happy. We done work in hour. You watch dance. Then, we go to Rosco's."

The Vietnamese manager again chattered something to Ping and pointed at the stage. The pretty Asian dancer chattered back and then made her way back up to the stage.

Aaron and Anderson bought a couple beers and were soon seated below the area where Ping was dancing. Aaron leaned back and smiled as she swayed to the music.

Soon after Ping took her break, Hue came running out in a very skimpy "police-woman" outfit and was hugging Anderson, much to the aggravation of the manager, who again began to chatter in Vietnamese and point to the stage.

Ping came back out in a different skimpy outfit a few minutes later. The two then danced on stage in front of Aaron and Anderson until their shift ended.

The four left the club and were soon packed in the back seat of a taxi headed to Rosco's Place.

Ping sat on Aaron's lap in the small car and snuggled up to him.

"Why you take so long? I may go to other GI if you not come back soon."

187

Aaron smiled and kissed her neck, causing her to smile.

"I told you, I had some training."

At this point, Anderson broke in, "Yeah, he's a medic now, Ping. I told him not to do it."

"You what now?" she asked, looking at him with concern.

"A medic, it's kind of like a doctor."

"You doctor now? Good, you doctor me tonight, sweetheart." She then snuggled him again as the taxi pulled into the lot at Rosco's Place.

Stepping out of the car and into the tropical heat, rock and roll came from inside the club.

After paying the cab driver, Anderson walked over and opened the large Asian-style door. A cloud of cigarette smoke billowed out.

Venturing inside, Aaron spotted a band on stage, one he was familiar with. The band was made up of American "grunts" or foot soldiers and had named the group "Infantry."

This club had a mix of men and women, as opposed to the club where Ping and Hue worked.

As the four made their way closer to the band, which was playing a popular Rolling Stones song, Aaron spotted a table occupied by the group's girlfriends.

They maneuvered to the band's table as the song ended.

"Well, look at this. The cavalry finally showed up!"

Aaron glanced up on stage as the lead singer had obviously spotted the four. He waved at the singer, as they were still trying to reach the table.

"Hey Spider, how's America? We haven't been there for a while now," the singer asked in a monotone voice. Laughter rang out from the crowd as the four finally made it to the table.

"It's still there!" Aaron shouted as he pulled a chair out for Ping. More laughter came from the crowd.

Several attractive Vietnamese women in miniskirts similar to the ones Ping and Hue wore examined them as they sat down at the table.

"Well, that's good to know, Spider," the singer said. He then took a drink of his beer as Aaron sat down.

"Well, now that you've sat down, how would you like to give Joe here a break?"

The singer then turned to the bass player, "You want a break, Joe?"

The bass player smiled. "As long as I can sit with Spider's girl."

More laughter erupted.

"You hear that, Spider? Come on up here so Joe can get some flirting in on Ping."

Aaron glanced at Ping, and she motioned for him to go up.

"Order me a beer, would you?" Aaron asked her as he stood back up.

"Yeah, sure. If Joe no steal me from you!"

Aaron gave her a suspicious glare as he left the table. She smiled seductively.

Joe stepped off the stage and immediately sat down by Ping.

Once Aaron had reached the stage, he squinted from the bright lights, and looking out to where Ping sat, he shouted, "Hey, just talking, Joe. Nothing else!"

There was more laughter as Joe yelled back, "Sure, Spider. Whatever you say, man!" He then put his arm over the back of Ping's chair and leaned over to talk with her.

As soon as Aaron had the strap to the bass guitar over his shoulder, the band started a lively rock and roll tune. The crowd shouted out in approval, and Aaron joined in.

Five songs later, Aaron stepped off the stage and, after some coaxing, managed to pry Joe away from Ping. Joe then stepped back on the stage, and the band began to play again.

Around midnight, the club closed. Aaron, Ping, Hue and Anderson found themselves staggering down the dark street, with a beer in each hand.

Seeing a light on in a shop ahead of them, they walked toward it.

A few seconds later, they found themselves in front of a tattoo parlor. Inside, the Vietnamese tattoo artist was finishing up on a soldier.

"Come on, Bones. Let's get one."

Aaron glanced at his friend. "I'm not getting an army tattoo, Anderson."

"You don't have to. I'll get one. You can get whatever you want, but you said six months ago that you'd get one if I did, remember?"

Aaron grimaced a bit, then tipped up his beer and finished it. Ping immediately handed him an unopened one and, taking the empty, sat it on the ground beside the wall.

"What do you think?" Aaron asked Ping.

"I no care what you do. I not get tattoo. It not good for my work. Not many tips for a tattoo girl."

"Come on, Bones. Let's go," Anderson started toward the door.

"Hey, my boyfriend is no Bones. He Spider. You stop call him Bones. I don like it." Ping then followed Hue, who had followed Anderson into the parlor.

Aaron shook his head but followed the other three in.

Ten minutes later, Aaron was sipping his warm beer and watching Anderson get a "1st cavalry" tattoo on his right upper arm.

Since the tattoo Anderson got was common, it didn't take long. Soon, his friend was looking the new artwork over. He then pulled his shirt back on and tapped Aaron's arm.

"Your turn, Bones."

"Hey, it Spider. I tell you already, Andreson!" Ping again protested and then took hold of Aaron's arm.

"Ping, you need to lighten up."

The Vietnamese woman stood up and slapped Anderson's chest, causing him to step back and laugh.

"You lighten up, Andreson!"

After both calmed down, Anderson shrugged his shoulders to Aaron, "Well?"

"Yeah, all right. But I'm not getting a first cav tattoo."

Ping turned to him. "You should get 'Spider' tattoo. I like Spider name."

"No, Bones. You know, with a medic cross!" Anderson said with enthusiasm.

Ping immediately stood up again and slapped him on the arm where he had just received the tattoo, causing him to flinch and put his hand over it.

"I toll you, Spider, not Bones!"

Hue laughed at the excitement.

"Ping, it needs to be Bones. He's a medic now."

"No! Spider!" Ping replied with a loud voice.

"Bones!"

"Spider!"

"Bones! Ping, come on!"

"Spider!" she said again.

Aaron sat listening. Then, he held up his hand, and both turned to him.

"How about, Spider Bones, no, Spider, but spelled with a Y instead of an I. Spyder Bones. With a medic cross and a spider web, somewhere on it."

Ping and Anderson looked at each other. Then, they looked at Aaron.

"Yeah, that sounds groovy." Anderson finally said.

Aaron looked at Ping.

"Yeah, that fine. But Spyder first, right?"

Aaron smiled and nodded.

After ten minutes of talking with the tattoo artist, a design was drawn up. It was a medic cross, and in a circular fashion, over the top and bottom were Spyder and Bones. In the corners of the cross, there were spider webs and one small spider.

After another hour in the tattoo chair, the four walked out of the parlor as Aaron pulled his shirt back on.

By now, it was close to 2:30AM. Aaron and Ping parted ways with Anderson and Hue.

On the way to Ping's grandmother's house, she kissed him almost nonstop. On several occasions, Aaron pulled her hand from his crotch as the taxi driver glanced in the mirror.

A few blocks from her grandmother's house, Aaron paid the cab driver as Ping rubbed his buttocks. Turning and walking in the darkness, they made their way along a path through foliage and humid heat to the small house.

Aaron had never asked Ping about her parents or why she lived with her blind grandmother. He wasn't sure if her parents were still alive or if she was just taking care of her elderly grandmother. Ping also never volunteered the information.

As they crept closer to the house, both became hushed, to avoid disturbing her grandmother.

Slowly, they moved toward the small structure, which had only a dim light shining in the front.

When they were about twenty feet from the house, a voice came from the darkness.

"Nghe này, một người lính của ánh sáng đến gần. Cái ác sẽ sợ và qua đời sẽ rơi vào quỷ bóng tối ai dám trespass. Là các quân nhân dũng cảm của ánh sáng, phải dũng cảm."

Both stopped in their tracks. It was Ping's grandmother. Suddenly, Aaron recalled that she said this every time he came to the house. He had asked Ping about it before, but she would never tell him what her grandmother was saying.

Now, Ping took Aaron by the hand and walked to the

193

house. She greeted her grandmother, who was sitting outside in the dark, and then led Aaron through the house and to her small room in the back.

"What did she say?" Aaron asked as Ping closed the door behind them.

"It nothing. No worry. She a little crazy is all."

Ping then grabbed Aaron's crotch and began to kiss him again. With some effort, Aaron pulled Ping from him.

"No. Wait, Ping. I've been away for over three months. You said your grandmother is blind, which I believe because we just walked up in almost total darkness. But your grandmother says the same thing every time I come to this house. Now, I need to know what she's saying."

Ping huffed. She then moved over and clicked on a small, dim lamp that sat on a table beside her bed.

She stared at Aaron for a few seconds, then replied.

"Spyder... I tell you already. She a little crazy. Just forget it." She then moved over and again reached for his crotch.

Aaron caught her hand before she took hold of him.

"Ping, I really want to know. You always put me off when I ask you. I want to know."

The Vietnamese woman grimaced, then ran her fingers through her jet-black hair.

A few seconds later, she pulled the straps of her short outfit over her shoulders. Then, she pulled it down to reveal her breasts.

"Don you want to know about these? You been gone for long time. Don't you miss these?"

Aaron glanced at her exposed breasts. He smiled slightly.

"Ping, you're stalling."

"Aaahhhhggg," she pulled her dress back up over her breasts. "You American, why you must know everything?"

As she sat on her bed, Aaron raised his arms, "I don't want to know everything, sweetheart. It's just that every time I come here, your grandmother says the same thing. Now, how does she know it's me, and why does she say the same thing? If it happened to you, wouldn't you be curious?"

Ping glanced up to him. She frowned but then said, "Look, Spyder, my grandmother was some kind of... I don know how to say."

Aaron thought about it. "What?"

Her face twisted in thought. "I don know. She...when she was young, she, see future things. The people, they pay her to see these future things."

"You mean, like a fortune-teller?"

Ping's face again twisted. "I don know what you say. She just sees things, like future things, things in spirit world. This is how she make money. She tells people what things they can do to stop from being hurt and things like that."

Aaron considered this.

"So, what's that got to do with what she's saying?" Aaron asked.

"It just crazy talk. I think she just talking like she is telling someone things from when she tells future things."

Aaron studied Ping. She looked at him and grunted with frustration.

"Nghe này, một người lính của ánh sáng đến gần. Cái ác sẽ sợ và qua đời sẽ rơi vào quỷ bóng tối ai dám trespass. Là các quân nhân dũng cảm của ánh sáng, phải dũng cảm.

"It mean, like, uhmm... Look! A soldier of light come near. Evil surely fear and death fall on dark...uhm... demons that... uhm, who dare trespass. Be brave, soldier of light. Be brave."

Aaron examined Ping. She looked at him.

"It crazy talk. I tol you. Right?"

For several seconds Aaron considered what she said. Ping watched him closely. Then, he turned to her.

"What were you showing me a few minutes ago?"

Ping gave him a sultry smile and pulled her dress down again. Soon, they were making love.

CHAPTER TWO:

Valley of the Dead

The following week, Aaron found himself in the jungle, getting shot at by the Vietcong. Initially, he had the urge to shoot back, but he soon adjusted to his new role as a combat medic.

While not in the field, Aaron tended a variety of wounds and ailments.

He always looked forward to time off and seeing Ping again. He would spend hours watching the exotic Asian beauty dance. Then, they would go to Rosco's Place, where he would often stand in for the bass player of the regular band. Afterward, they would try to sneak into her grandmother's house. Regardless of it being day or night, the blind elderly Asian woman would greet him with the familiar, though cryptic, greeting.

Before he knew it, his leave or pass would be over, and he would be back in the thick of a firefight.

"You got a smoke, Bones?" Private Wilson glanced at Aaron and then refocused on the dense jungle in front of him.

"I don't smoke."

"Oh yeah," the young private replied, and then lifted his M-16 up a little higher, as if ready for anything.

"Since when did you start smoking?" Aaron asked the young man as they pushed through a leafy bush.

"A few weeks ago."

"Well, I don't think it's very good for you," Aaron replied.

"Maybe not, but getting shot at ain't either."

Aaron smiled a bit, "I suppose that's true."

They walked for another five minutes. Suddenly, bullets began to fly all around them. Immediately, the soldiers dropped to the ground. The men in the forward positions began to return fire.

Aaron crawled over to a young private who had been hit in the leg. He was holding it and rocking back and forth in pain.

As Aaron began to help the wounded soldier, he could hear the lieutenant calling for air support on the radio.

Leaves and brush from the trees above fell all around as the bullets continued to pierce the air.

The lieutenant turned and yelled to a soldier with the grenade launcher, "In sixty seconds, plant a couple smoke grenades in their position. I don't want them bastards to have time to get out! Air support will be here any time now!"

Aaron glanced over to the soldier, who nodded and began loading a smoke grenade in the launcher.

In the forward position, the chattering of the M-60 machine gun began to sound off.

Aaron patted the wounded man after giving him a shot of morphine and quickly putting a bandage on his leg. He then began to crawl over to another wounded soldier who was calling out for a medic.

As he pulled a bandage pack from his gear, he could hear the grenade launcher going off with a "phthunk." Four times the soldier launched smoke grenades into the enemy's lines.

The bullets stopped just about the time he could hear the Hueys flying toward them.

Staying low, Aaron crouched over the soldier, who was now almost screaming in pain. The choppers flew overhead and launched rockets into the enemy positions. Then machine gun fire came as the Huey gunners strafed the area.

It was a long day as he and the wounded were evacuated from the area by helicopter. Back at the base, he continued to administer aid. An hour later, more of his comrades arrived. They had continued the firefight after he left and, along with a medic who stayed, were finally airlifted out of the area.

Around 10:00PM, Aaron shuffled through the humid night air and finally reached his tent. Anderson was laying on his cot but leaned up on his elbow as Aaron pulled some clothes from his locker.

"Burning the midnight oil?" Anderson asked.

Aaron threw a towel over his arm and, along with his clothes and shaving kit, turned toward the door.

"Yeah, and then some," he replied.

"Hey," Anderson said just before Aaron left the tent.

"What? I need a shower and some sleep."

"It was like the Vietcong was waiting for us today. It's like someone is telling them where we're going to be, and they just wait for us. You know what I mean?"

Aaron nodded his head a little. "Yeah, I agree. But don't look at me. I didn't tell them."

He then walked outside into the dark and toward the dimly lit showers. Anderson lit a cigarette and laid back on his cot.

The following weekend, the two were sitting at a table in front of the stage where Ping and Hue danced.

Aaron finished the remainder of his beer. He then looked up and smiled at Ping as she swayed about and watched him. Soldiers yelled out and whistled at the barely dressed dancers on stage.

A few hours later, they were at Rosco's Place. Later, Aaron rented a room for the night, as they didn't want to go all the way back to Ping's grandmother's house.

This routine continued for seven months. It was a strange existence that revolved around danger, death and love. Aaron thought little about other things. He survived to spend another weekend with Ping. He seldom considered the possibility of everything changing. But it soon would.

"Damn, it's hot here!" Private Wilson wiped the sweat from his forehead and then put his helmet back on.

Aaron nodded but kept his eyes on the trees that were about thirty-five yards on the other side of the field they were moving across. He didn't like the situation. He could see the lieutenant ahead, and he seemed nervous.

"Don't you think it's hot, Bones?" Wilson persisted and then took a seemingly desperate drag from his cigarette.

"Yeah, it's hot," Aaron replied, still scanning the woodland area across the field.

"Shh. Keep it down back there." The lieutenant then motioned with his hand behind him.

This was a bad place to be. Aaron felt his stomach turn as they continued across the field. He hated these situations. It was way too...out in the open.

Cautiously, they continued toward the woodlands on the other side.

Then, he heard a "phlunnk" sound. He knew what it was and dropped to the ground just as the bullets started to fly. The lieutenant yelled, "HIT THE DIRT!"

Private Wilson was hit in the leg and the arm before he could get down. The split second of Aaron knowing the sound of a mortar shell being dropped in the tube and Private Wilson not knowing, was the difference between getting shot and not.

As the bullets took down five or six men, the mortar rounds began to fall.

Explosions rocked the earth Aaron was attempting to claw into.

There were not many low spaces, but Aaron managed to slither to a lower area.

An M-60 machine gunner began returning fire. Men were screaming, and Aaron quickly counted seven wounded.

As the return fire slowed the enemy's mortar attacks, Aaron moved over to Private Wilson and took hold of his uniform. He was screaming out in pain. Aaron pulled him over to the low area.

"Where's my gawd damn M79? Can someone plant some

grenades on them bastards?" The lieutenant yelled out just before another mortar shell landed close by.

Aaron left Private Wilson and crawled over to where the M79 gunner had been. He found half of him lying face up, dead eyes staring into space.

Fortunately, the mortar round had not destroyed the grenade launcher. Aaron quickly pulled it from the dead soldier, along with his ammo bag.

As fast as he could, Aaron loaded the weapon and soon had a grenade headed to the wooded area across the field. He loaded another round and another. As they hit, he adjusted his aim to where he thought the enemy mortars were.

"I need air support at whiskey 527, repeat whiskey 527. We have casualties. We need fire support and med-evacs!" The lieutenant was almost shouting on the radio as Aaron continued to fire the M79.

As more soldiers fired into the woods and more grenades landed in the enemy's positions, the return fire slowed.

Soon, they heard the Hueys, and the enemy seemed to back away. As the air support fired into the woods, Aaron began tending to the wounded.

Sporadic small arms fire came into the area as several helicopters landed to extract the wounded.

Anderson was firing his M16 into the woodlands to keep the Vietcong from attacking again.

Smoke drifted around the men. Aaron came to Private Wilson. He had lost a lot of blood and was fading out.

More helicopters came in and landed.

"Everyone out! Get the hell out! We'll let air support clean them bastards up!" the lieutenant yelled out as the others loaded into a Huey.

Aaron lifted Private Wilson and carried him over to a Huey. Enemy bullets hit several spots on the helicopter as Aaron hoisted the young man up. A crewman helped Wilson into the last available seat.

"Come on!" the crewman yelled.

Aaron jumped up on the skid and leaning half in and half out of the chopper. It lifted off. Vietcong bullets hit the skid of the helicopter, coming very close to Aaron's foot. The Huey gunner sprayed M-60 machinegun fire around the woodlands.

The Huey climbed higher into the air. Aaron glanced back and saw another helicopter about twenty yards away. The machine gunner was also laying down a stream of M-60 rounds into the wooded area.

Private Wilson began to stir. He moaned from the pain and moved to his right, almost pushing Aaron out of the helicopter. He took hold of the seat and tried to shift over some. Bullets again hit the helicopter. Aaron could see in the cockpit, and as he was trying to get a better hold, he saw one of the pilots get hit. The pilot slumped to the side, and the helicopter suddenly leaned. Aaron lost the slight grip he had on the seat and fell backward from the Huey. His heart began to race as he and the helicopter separated.

Arms flailing about, he seemed to be falling slowly as his mind raced. In these brief seconds, he did something extraordinary. He somehow leaped from himself, just as his body impacted the ground.

How he did it, Aaron didn't know, but as soon as he hit the ground, part of his body, the upper part, was somewhere else.

His heart beat fiercely as he seemed to be half on the ground in Vietnam, and half in a place he could barely comprehend.

Looking around, it was as if he were hanging from his midsection on a massive glimmering wall. He could see the other part of his body through this strange glistening barrier, but he was caught between the two places.

Aaron looked down and suddenly became even more frightened. Below was what could only be described as a nightmarish hell. There were black, evil-looking lizard creatures eating and fighting over what appeared to be bodies of people.

Then, to his side, something began to slip through the glistening wall. Aaron felt nauseous as what appeared to be a rotten and diseased person slithered through the barrier. The person looked to be alive, though only barely. Then, Aaron realized it was a soldier from his unit. The man was not a friend of his, but he could see it was him.

As the man's dying eyes stared at Aaron, his black and infested body fell through the wall and then onto the bottom where the grotesque demon-looking creatures waited. As soon as the body landed, the creatures began to devour it.

Aaron tried to move through the wall and back to the world he knew, but he was stuck. As he struggled, farther away from him, a bright light burst through the wall. It shot like a bolt of light across the area and above the demon creatures.

As Aaron watched, he noticed strange beasts and beings flying about in what looked to be the sky, though there was no sun or clouds to be seen.

From what he could see, there were two types of creatures. One was radiating light and appeared to have shining armor. The other was a dreadful-looking black creature with the appearance of a gargoyle.

These beings flew about and often attacked one another in midair. The strangeness again caused a streak of fear to strike his heart. Aaron once again tried to move through the glimmering wall.

As he looked to where his lower body and legs would be, on the other side of the odd, shimmering barrier, he observed soldiers picking him up. Behind them were several more Huey helicopters.

As they carried his body to the chopper, a thin thread-like substance streamed away from the wall. It was as if a thread of his clothing was attached to the part of him that was on the other side of the wall, spooling out as the soldiers carried him.

Again, he struggled in his apparent trapped situation. Then, a large, hideous gargoyle creature landed about fifteen feet from him.

Aaron's eyes widened as the creature stared at him, then began to walk, as if it were not sideways but walking on a floor or the ground.

The creature extended its arms and claws to take hold of Aaron. Suddenly, one of the light-radiating beings landed in front of Aaron. With one stroke of a shining sword, the being sliced the gargoyle in two, and it fell to the hellish depths below.

The being then turned and examined Aaron closely. It was the most beautiful woman Aaron had ever seen. He thought for certain this must be an angel. She had wings and wore a golden set of armor.

As she leaned closer and studied Aaron, he noticed her left eye was a baby-blue color, and her right eye was a beautiful cream color.

Another gargoyle creature landed close by. The angelic being turned and began to fight. As this was happening, Aaron saw more disgusting, diseased bodies slipping through the glimmering wall. They would fall to the ground where the black lizard creatures would descend upon them. As they ate the bodies, the mouths of these people would scream in terror. It seemed to Aaron, these people had died, yet they were somewhat aware of their hell-like situations, at least until the creatures had finished with them.

At the same time, there would be brilliant bolts of light from the wall. Some were close to Aaron, and others appeared to be miles away. These light bolts would streak across the sky, never dropping into the blackness of the ground.

While the angel and the gargoyle fought, another angel landed and then another. Soon, another gargoyle landed and began attacking the angelic beings.

Once the first angel had struck down the gargoyle she was fighting, she turned to Aaron. Again, he was captivated by her eyes. She paid no attention to this, and with her free hand, she reached inside his upper body, penetrating the very flesh itself. He was shocked and frightened as he looked down to see her hand inside his upper body. He could feel it as well, yet there was no pain.

After doing something inside his upper body, the angel extracted her hand, took hold of him, and pulled him away from the wall. He was horrified to see there was only half of him in her arms as she took flight.

As she flew from the wall, Aaron noticed a thin thread streaming from his body, very similar to what he saw when the medics carried his body away on the other side of the wall. He could also feel a strange sensation inside but could think of no words to describe the feeling.

As the angel flew swiftly, carrying him over the black, evil-looking creatures on the ground, he felt a horror and dark, empty sadness that was as he had never felt. Then, more gargoyles swooped in close and began attacking the angel as she carried him.

He looked back and saw other angels were fighting the gargoyles as they tried to get to him as well as the thin thread streaming from him.

Suddenly, Aaron began to cry. He sensed the evil that lay below him and the danger his very being was now in, and it became completely overwhelming. Tears streamed down his face as if he were a small child.

Again and again, the evil gargoyle creatures would attack, appearing very desperate to take Aaron from the angelic woman. Again and again, angels would repel the creatures.

Through tear-soaked eyes, Aaron could see more and more angels and gargoyles also fighting all around the thin thread streaming from his half body. The battle stretched back for what looked to be miles. It seemed to be a frenzied fight by the gargoyles to take Aaron or take hold of the thread streaming from his being.

All along this thread, the struggle was intensifying as more and more angels, as well as gargoyles, joined in. Aaron could not imagine what would happen to him if the gargoyles reached the thread.

Then, unexpectedly, he and the angel carrying him entered a bright area of light. When this happened, the thin thread instantly became light as well. When the thread became illuminated, the angels stopped fighting and let the gargoyles fly to it. Several of the evil beings tried to stop themselves but could not turn back fast enough. As the creatures flew into the thread, they were sliced in two, as if the thread had become a brilliant razor.

After viewing this, Aaron lost awareness.

When he woke, Aaron found himself sitting in a chair. Raising his head, he saw the recreation room at his barracks in Fort Hood, Texas.

Aaron looked around, and there was no one to be seen. The television in front of him was turned on, but it had a black and white, snowy screen and white noise.

For several seconds, Aaron examined his surroundings. Although he was familiar with this place, it was apparent there was something very different. The light was all around, yet there seemed to be no source. Looking up, he noticed there were no light fixtures in the ceiling.

As he looked back down, a man was sitting in the chair across from him and to the right of the TV. Aaron was astounded that he didn't jump from the shock of someone suddenly being where there was no one before. But, oddly, he wasn't afraid at all.

The man wore army fatigues, and Aaron noticed he had the rank of captain.

Standing quickly, Aaron came to attention and saluted the officer.

"At ease," the captain said, with a low, authoritative voice that sounded almost as if it were coming from an amplifier.

Aaron changed his stance to "at ease."

"Please, sit down, soldier," the captain said.

Aaron sat back down.

For several seconds, the two simply looked at each other. Then Aaron spoke.

"Sir, I'm confused. I don't understand how I got here. Have I lost my memory, or what?"

"Well, what do you remember?" the officer asked.

"I was in Vietnam. We were attacked by the Vietcong. Huey helicopters came, and we were bugging out. I was sort of in one, but not all the way. The pilot was hit, and the chopper tilted. I fell out. It must have been forty or fifty feet from the ground. Then, when I hit..."

Aaron stopped as the very strange memories came back to him. The captain studied him.

"Then what?" the captain asked.

Aaron looked around again. He sensed for certain now that he wasn't at Fort Hood. But it looked so real.

"Then, some very strange memories. I don't know. Maybe I was dreaming."

"You weren't dreaming."

Aaron looked at the captain. Again, he felt that he should be shocked. But he still felt calm.

"When our guardians found you, the death wraiths were very close to taking you. Fortunately, they were able to get you here. Otherwise, you might have found yourself in the depths of the underworld, where the remainder of your soul would have been sucked dry by the dwellers of that unspeakable region."

Once again, Aaron felt oddly calm upon hearing this horrific possibility.

"I don't, uhm… Where am I, sir?"

"You're in an area that is between the physical world and, well, another realm of existence that we call the second realm. It could be described as a very small, isolated area on the edge of the spiritual realm, perhaps like a small island."

Aaron strained at the idea. "Do you mean purgatory?"

"Well, it is likely what some have described as purgatory. But it's not the purgatory that many have written of. Though it certainly may have been identified as such.

"You're in a place that is necessary for the balance of interactions between the physical and spiritual realms."

After some thought, Aaron replied. "I didn't know there was a place in the spiritual realm that looked like Fort Hood."

The captain smiled. "Actually, it looks like a place that your mind can understand and relate to. For someone else, it would look completely different. Your mind devised this 'spiritual Fort Hood' for you to relate to and understand what the mind cannot really comprehend."

Once again, Aaron considered the information. Finally, after a few seconds of thought, he asked, "How did I get here? I mean, why am I here? Am I alive or dead?"

"You're what might be called both alive and dead. In the physical world, you're in a comatose state. Here, you're alive and well, but in an environment that is not hospitable to your physical being.

"As to why and how you got here, you are undoubtedly what would be called a 'unique case,' an anomaly, if you will. It's not uncommon for people to find their way here. But they do so in a spiritual sense. It often takes years of training to enter this realm. When done so by the spiritual method, these people move across the sphere of death as if they were vapor. Their presence is not perceived by the gatekeepers of the dead.

"However, you entered the realm in a rare manner. Your spirit, or soul, left your body at the instant of what would have been death. So, what happened is you didn't die, but you didn't live either. Thus, you're here."

Aaron's eyes squinted as he considered this.

"So, what happens now?"

"That's a good question. Much of what happens now is up to you," the captain replied.

"How is it up to me? I don't understand." Aaron shook his head in disbelief. "I don't understand any of this."

"The fact that you are here now means you do have the ability to understand. Not only can you understand, but you can utilize the information here as well as in the physical world. Due to your unique situation, you have potential far beyond the others who come here for training and wisdom."

After saying this, the captain stood and walked over to the pool table. He picked up a pool stick and began shooting balls into the pockets.

Aaron stood and walked over to the table. He watched the captain for a few seconds, then asked him, "How do I understand this, and how do I change it?"

The captain looked at him and asked, "Until you understand it, how do you know if you want to change it?"

Aaron thought about this as the captain shot another ball into the corner pocket. Then, seeming to sense Aaron was struggling, he laid the pool cue on the table.

"You were fighting in a war when you crossed the plane of existence. You should now sense there is another war, a war that has been raging since the dawn of time, a war that mankind is involved with, though only on a small scale. For the most part, mankind is still the equivalent of a spiritual child, perhaps, like a teenager. They think they've got it all figured out and know so much, but this is, in fact, the very attitude that keeps them from seeing more, from growing beyond the barriers they face."

Suddenly, Aaron's days in Sunday school and church service began to come back.

"The war between God and Satan," he said, almost to himself.

"Yes, you know about the war," the captain said.

"I heard the stories in Sunday school. I remember sermons our pastor gave. But they all seemed like ancient history. I believed them, but it seemed to be long ago and far away."

The captain walked over to the window. He glanced out and then turned to Aaron.

"It's a war that has been going on long before the earth or mankind was around. Your world is affected less than other worlds. Yet, the enemy would bring total darkness and death to all if it were ever victorious.

"Now, you must make a decision. You must decide if you will fight for good or return to your world and allow natural laws to take their course.

"Or, there is one other option; death."

Aaron walked over to the window next to the captain. Looking out, he saw a small squad of soldiers doing exercises.

"Who are they?" Aaron asked.

"They're soldiers of light. Few can make it here. Fewer still can endure the training needed to be functional in the physical world. Those are the few that have made it past the initial trials. Their training will begin soon."

There were eleven soldiers in a small parade area. Soon, they were called into formation, and what appeared to be a sergeant inspected them and dismissed the group.

"Are they like me?" Aaron asked.

"No, not entirely. They've reached this place through meditation. They're here spiritually, but their bodies are in the physical realm. They've not crossed the valley of the dead in the same manner as you are."

"So, if I choose to let nature run its course, what will happen?" Aaron asked.

"I don't know. You'll be returned, and depending on your ability to recover, you will live or die. The laws of nature follow their own path. It's the way the creator intended, and regardless of what some may say, it's a sufficient system."

"And, if I choose to fight for good, what does that mean?" Aaron asked.

"It means you will choose the most difficult path. You will endure extensive training here. Then, the real trials will start when you return to the physical realm. The life of a soldier of light is not an easy one. You will encounter and combat evil that most men don't understand or even believe exists. There will be few in the physical realm that can assist you in your battles. However, you will have an understanding that what you're doing is of a higher good, much nobler than the war you were fighting in the physical sense."

Aaron walked over and sat back down, expelling a long breath of air.

"I'm no hero—not like that."

The captain also sat down across from him.

"Actually, you are who you are. Deep down, you know who you are. And if you were not that kind of hero, you would not be here. You chose something other than dying. You chose to find a place that you could be who you are. You've known for some time now that you were different. What you must do now is either accept who you are or lose faith in something you've felt for a long time."

When the captain said this, Aaron suddenly saw the truth. It was there all along. He had always known it deep in his soul.

The sudden revelation caused a tear to erupt from Aaron's eye. He asked, "What must I do?"

"You know that as well. Before you can do anything else, you must repent and be cleansed."

Aaron immediately fell to his knees and repented. As he arose, he became a complete person. He knew who he was and what the creator had intended him to be.

"Get some rest," the captain then said. Aaron went to his room. It was just as he recalled from Fort Hood. Everything was the same, except he had no roommate. He climbed into his bunk, and sleep quickly overcame him.

Thanks for reading the preview of Spyder Bones. For your convenience we've listed additional Oliver Phipps books you may be interested in.

For a complete listing please check out all of Oliver Phipps' works online.

The House on Cooper Lane:
Based on a True Story

It's 1984, and all Bud Fisher wants to do is to find a place to live in Madison Louisiana. He and his dog Badger discover a beautiful old mansion that was converted into apartments.

Something should have felt odd when he found nobody lived in any of the apartments. To make matters worse, the owner was reluctant to let him rent one. Eventually he negotiates an apartment in the historic old house, but soon finds out that he's not quite as alone as he thought. What ghostly secret has the owner failed to share?

It's up to Bud to unravel the mysteries of the upstairs apartments, but is he ready to find out the truth?

A Tempest Soul

Seventeen-year-old Gina Falcone has been alone for most of her life. Her father passed away while she was young, and her un-affectionate mother eventually leaves her to care for herself when she was only thirteen.

Though her epic journey begins by an almost deadly mistake, Gina will find many of her heart's desires in the most unlikely of places. The loss of everything is the catalyst that brings her to an unimagined level of accomplishment in her life.

However, Gina, soon realizes it is the same events that brought her success that may also bring everything crashing down around her. The new life she has built soon beckons for something she left behind. Now, the new woman must find a way to dance through a life she could have never dreamt of.

Where the Strangers Live

When a passenger plane disappeared over the Indian Ocean in autumn 2013, a massive search gets underway.

A deep trolling, unmanned pod picks up faint readings, and soon the deep-sea submersible Oceana and her three crew members are four miles below the ocean surface in search of the black box from flight N340.

Nothing could have prepared the submersible crew for what they discover and what happens afterward. Ancient evils and other world creatures challenge the survival of the Oceana's crew. Mysteries of the past are revealed, and death hangs in the balance for Sophie, Troy and Eliot in this deep-sea Science Fiction thriller.

Twelve Minutes till Midnight

A man catches a ride on a dusty Louisiana road, only to find out he's traveling with notorious outlaws Bonnie and Clyde.

The suspense is nonstop as confrontation settles in, between a man determined to stand on truth, and an outlaw determined to dislocate him from it.

"Twelve Minutes till Midnight will take you on an unforgettable ride."

Diver Creed Station

Wars, diseases, and a massive collapse of civilization have ravaged the human-race of a hundred years in the future. Finally, in the late twenty-second century, mankind slowly begins to struggle back from the edge of extinction.

When a huge "virtual life" facility is restored from a hibernation type of storage and slowly brought back online, a new hope materializes.

Fragments of humanity begin to move into the remnants of Denver and the Virtua-Gauge facilities, which offer seven days of virtual leisure for seven days work in this new and growing social structure.

Most inhabitants of this new lifestyle begin to hate the real world, and work for the seven-day period inside the virtual pods. It's the variety of luxury role play inside the virtual zone that supply's the incentive needed to work hard for seven days in the real world.

In this new social structure, a man can work for seven days in a food dispersal unit and earn seven days as a twenty-first century software billionaire in the virtual zone. As time goes by, and more of the virtual pods are brought back online life appears to be getting better.

Rizette and her husband Oray are young technicians that settle into their still-new marriage as the virtual facilities expand and thrive.

Oray has recently attained the level of a Class A Diver and enjoys his job. The Divers are skilled technicians that perform critical repairs to the complex system, from inside the virtual zone.

His occupation as a Diver demands constant work in the secure "lower levels" of the system. These highly secure areas are the dividing space between the real world and the world of the virtual zone. When the facility was built, the original designers intentionally placed this buffer zone in the programming to avoid threats from non-living virtual personnel.

As Oray becomes more experienced in his elite technical position as a Diver, he is approached by his virtual assistant and forced to make a difficult decision. Oray's decision triggers events that soon pull him and his wife Rizette into a deadly quest for survival.

The stage becomes a massive and complex maze of virtual world sequences, as escape or entrapment hang on precious threads of information.

System ghosts from the distant past, intermingle with mysterious factions that have thrown Oray and Rizette into a cyberspace trap with little hope for survival.

Ghosts of Company K:
Based on a True Story

Tag along with young Bud Fisher during his daily adventures in this ghostly tale based on actual events. It's 1971 and Bud and his family move into an old house in Northern Arkansas. Bud soon discovers they live not far from a very interesting cave and a historic Civil War battle site. As odd things start to happen, Bud tries to solve the mysteries, but soon the entire family experiences a haunting situation.

If you enjoy ghost tales based on true events, then you'll enjoy Ghosts of Company K. This heartwarming story brings the reader into the life and experiences of a young boy growing up in the early 1970s. Seen through innocent and unsuspecting eyes, Ghosts of Company K reveals a haunting tale from the often-unseen perspective of a young boy.

Bane of the Innocent

"There's no reason for them to shoot us; we ain't anyone" - Sammy, Bane of the Innocent.

Two young boys become unlikely companions during the fall of Atlanta. Sammy and Ben somehow find themselves, and each other, in the rapidly changing and chaotic environment of the war-torn Georgia City.

As the siege ends and the fall begins in late August and early September of 1864, the Confederate troops begin to move out, and Union forces cautiously move into the city. Ben and Sammy simply struggle to survive, but in the process, they develop a friendship that will prove more important than either could imagine.

A Life Naive

Life for twenty-seven-year-old Hershel Lawson has been relatively uneventful, and that's the way he likes it. When his grandmother passes away, leaving him her car and a last wish of him taking her ashes to L.A., his life takes a turn and it will never be the same again.

With his new task and grandmother's ashes, Hershel sets out from St. Louis Missouri in the spring of 1962. He travels unimpeded along scenic Route 66 for two days but is suddenly and unexpectedly relieved of two important things, his car and wallet.

Sally is a sassy and street-smart young woman on her way to Hollywood. She's determined to prove everyone wrong in the "one horse town" she left and be successful as an actress in California. Through mishaps of her own, Sally comes across Hershel. Though neither one realizes it, the real journey is about to begin.

Take a seat and journey with Hershel and Sally along historic Route 66 during its heyday. Laugh and maybe shed a tear or two as they struggle against the odds, and often each other, to make it a few more miles down the highway.

The Bitter Harvest

It's 1825, and a small Native American village has lost many of its people and bravest warriors to a pack of Lofa; huge beasts' humanoid in shape and covered with coarse hair. The creatures are taller than any normal man, and fiercer than even the wildest animal.

Rather than leave the land of their ancestors, the tribe chooses to stay and fight the beasts. But they're losing the war, and perhaps more critically, they're almost without hope.

The small community grasps for anything to help them survive. There is a warrior on the frontier known as Orenda. He's already legendary across the west for his bravery and honor.

Onsi, a young villager, sets out on a journey to find the warrior.

Orenda will be forced to choose between almost certain death, not just for himself, but also his warrior wife Nazshoni and her brother Kanuna, or a dishonorable refusal that would mean annihilation for the entire village.

The crucial decision is only the beginning, and Orenda will soon face the greatest test of his life; the challenge that could turn out to be too much even for a legendary warrior.

Spyder Bones

We've heard the tales. The eternal struggle between good and evil. Many religions are based on the concepts. God, Satan, angels and demons; ideals interwoven into our very existence.

Most people have chosen a side, whether they admit it to themselves or not. Many have at least a basic understanding of what is happening. Some have even discovered secrets beyond the veil of what we see. However, there are a few, who not only understand the war, but are in the very thick of it.

This is the story of Spyder Bones, a mystic warrior.

It's the summer of 1969 and Aaron Prescott is a seasoned soldier. After serving one tour of duty in Vietnam as a cavalryman, Aaron returns for a second tour as a combat medic.

Aaron's life revolves around the love of his Vietnamese girlfriend, the danger of combat, and his passion for music. It's not an overly complicated existence, but that's about to change.

Aaron, or Spyder as he is known to his friends, suffers a near death experience during combat. He is subsequently trapped in a comatose state for months. During this time, he is exposed to an unseen war. A spiritual struggle that most people only have a vague awareness of.

Aaron must make some difficult decisions, but, regardless of anything else, he knows his life will never be the same.

www.ingramcontent.com/pod-product-compliance
Lightning Source LLC
Chambersburg PA
CBHW070813120626
46556CB00002B/485